FOREVER AND ALWAYS SERIES - BOOK 2

NORA BLOOM

Chapter One

LISA

L isa Montgomery wove through the tables of the Seabreeze Café with practiced agility, her hands expertly balancing a tray of freshly baked muffins. Sunlight spilled across the rustic wooden floors, bathing the room in a golden hue that promised a new day full of possibilities. The scent of roasted coffee beans mingled with the sweet aroma of pastries, setting a comforting stage for the early risers who would soon filter through the door, seeking their morning solace.

As she aligned the chairs with a gentle nudge of her hip, Lisa glanced toward the adjoining woodwork shop, where handcrafted furniture and trinkets awaited the admiration of patrons. She tucked a loose strand of wavy brown hair behind her ear and exhaled a focused breath, willing her mind to stay on the tasks at hand despite the undercurrent of uncertainty that seemed to tug at her heart.

Every morning, Lisa's day began as a delicate

dance with the dawn, the rhythm led by the gentle cadence of the ocean just beyond her café's weathered door. She moved with practiced ease through the familiar motions, the scent of freshly ground coffee beans mingling with the salty tang of sea air. The café, an intimate haven crafted from her resilience and dreams, hummed quietly with the anticipation of the morning rush.

Outside, waves whispered secrets to the Alaskan shoreline, their hushed crashes a soothing soundtrack to Lisa's meticulous preparations. She filled the display case with an array of homemade pastries, each a testament to her dedication—the flaky crusts and sumptuous fillings arranged like jewels under the soft glow of the overhead lights. The aroma of cinnamon and vanilla swirled around her, a comforting embrace.

"Mom, are the pancakes ready?" Abigail's sleepy voice cut through the stillness of the pre-dawn calm, pulling Lisa back to the warmth of the kitchen. Lisa loved Saturdays when the kids had no school, and everything moved at a slower pace.

Lisa turned to find Ethan and Abigail shuffling into the room, their eyes half-lidded with remnants of sleep. Oliver and Lisa had recently moved their entire family into the apartment above the café, and now they were living there, all five of them, to better keep up with all the work. This way, the café was not just a workplace but their home. It was a big sacrifice since they all loved the house they lived in, especially the creek behind it and the view of the mountains. But it simply didn't function for them, and it was too expensive with two rent payments, so this way, they saved some money. It was just more practical.

Ethan's protective hand rested gently on his younger sister's shoulder, guiding her forward as if steering a ship through foggy waters.

"Almost there, my darlings," Lisa said, her voice a soft melody as she whisked the batter in the bowl with one hand while reaching to ruffle Ethan's short hair with the other. A smile graced her lips, reflecting the same warmth that danced in Abigail's wide, expectant eyes.

The sizzle of batter hitting the hot skillet filled the air, and Ethan perched himself on a stool at the counter, his green eyes following Lisa's every move with an attentiveness that belied his years. Abigail clambered up beside him, her curls bouncing with each movement, her laughter a tinkling bell that resonated in the cozy confines of the kitchen.

"Race you to see who finishes first!" Ethan challenged, his grogginess giving way to the spark of competition.

"Okay!" Abigail agreed eagerly, her giggles turning into peals of laughter as Lisa slid a golden-brown pancake onto each of their plates.

The homey scene was a delicate dance of love and routine, a daily performance that stitched together the fabric of their lives. As Lisa poured the syrup and watched her children dive into their breakfast, the thrill of the day ahead pulsed through her veins. It was a feeling tinged with suspense, for the unknowns that lay beyond the safety of these walls kept her ever vigilant, ever hopeful, and always prepared for what life might serve up next.

&

Ethan's fork clattered against the plate, his cheeks puffed out with the last bite of pancake as he declared victory. Abigail pouted playfully before breaking into a grin, her defeat easily forgotten in the joy of the moment. Lisa watched them, an affectionate smile playing on her lips. The sun spilled across the kitchen table, casting a halo over the children's heads, and for a fleeting moment, the world was perfect.

"Mom, look! I won!" Ethan exclaimed, his voice bubbling with pride.

"Abby's just letting you win," she teased him gently. Her eyes softened at the edges as they met the pair of sparkling orbs that mirrored her own resilience. Her heart swelled, filled to the brim with love for these two little souls who had weathered storms alongside her and still found reasons to laugh.

The creak of a floorboard pulled her gaze away from the children, and there stood Oliver, leaning against the doorframe with a weariness that seemed to hang on his shoulders like a heavy cloak. His dark hair was a disheveled testament to a night spent walking the halls with their young daughter.

"Morning," he murmured, his voice rough with fatigue.

"Hey," Lisa replied, the concern etched on her face softening as he crossed the kitchen to where she stood.

His arms enveloped her in a hug that felt like the safe harbor he so missed from his days at sea but had given up to help build the café and woodshop and to be there more for the family. He pressed his lips to her cheek, and it was a tender kiss that spoke volumes—of gratitude, shared struggles, and a bond that not even the relentless tides of life could break.

"Did Julia finally settle?" Lisa asked, her hands resting on his forearms, feeling the muscle beneath the worn flannel.

"Like a ship after a storm," Oliver said, a small smile finding its way through his exhaustion. "But every hour, she was up, wanting to see the stars or just to remind us she's captain now."

"Sounds about right." Lisa chuckled, her laughter mingling with the warmth of the morning light. She found solace in the rhythm of their life together—a symphony of sawdust, syrup, and the soft coos of a baby that wove through the essence of their home.

The corners of Lisa's eyes crinkled as she caught Oliver's gaze, a silent conversation passing between them. His hand found the small of her back—a touch that was both an anchor and a promise. They stood amidst the hum of the kitchen appliances and the soft patter of their children's feet, each glance acknowledging the delicate dance of their lives—balancing ledgers with laughter and coffee orders with cuddles.

Their connection was a quiet force, a shared

resilience against the tide of worry that often threatened to breach the walls they had carefully built around their family. The café, with its aroma of roasted beans and the comforting scent of wood shavings from the adjacent workshop, was more than just a business; it was a testament to their collective dreams and relentless determination.

But even within this cocoon of warmth they had spun together, reality loomed large in their periphery —a stack of bills, a whimpering child at night, and the ceaseless churn of responsibility that never quite ebbed.

It was in that moment of mutual understanding, a breath held in tandem, that the outside world beckoned once more. The front door chime sliced through their reverie, a sharp reminder that the day was in full swing.

Lisa turned toward the sound, her heart skipping a beat as if on cue, every sense heightened. The wooden floorboards creaked under the weight of new footsteps, a harbinger of the day's first patron seeking refuge in the sanctuary of her café.

"Good morning," she called out, her voice steady despite the fluttering in her chest. The customer, a regular whose name hovered on the tip of her tongue, offered a nod and a smile that didn't quite reach his tired eyes. He was a silhouette framed by the doorway, the golden sunlight casting his shadow long across the room.

"The usual?" Lisa asked, already reaching for the heavy ceramic mug that felt familiar in her grasp.

Her mind, however, remained alight with the unspoken words exchanged with Oliver, the thrill of uncertainty that lay hidden beneath each new day's surface.

§❧

Lisa's smile radiated warmth as she scribbled down the customer's order, her pen dancing across the notepad in a familiar rhythm. The rich aroma of coffee beans ground and brewed to perfection filled the air, mingling with the sweet scent of cinnamon from the freshly baked pastries on display. She chatted about the weather and the local high school's upcoming football game, her voice a soft melody above the gentle hum of conversation and clinking dishware.

"Make sure you try the cherry scone, Jerry. Baked them fresh this morning," she said, her eyes crinkling with genuine affection for the regulars who were as much a part of this place as the worn wooden counters.

Her attention flitted between the customer and the kitchen doorway where Ethan and Abigail hovered. Their laughter was a bright counterpoint to the morning's stillness, and Lisa felt a surge of love for the beautiful chaos that was her life.

Once Jerry settled at his usual table by the window with a contented sigh, Lisa seized a lull in the influx of patrons to slip into the back office. The tiny room was a quiet haven, bathed in the muted light filtering through blinds caked with sawdust—a testament to Oliver's late-night woodworking.

She eased into the chair, the leather creaking under her weight, and opened the ledger with hands that bore the evidence of her labor; faint stains of coffee and varnish intermingled on her skin. Her brow furrowed as she traced the columns of numbers, each digit an anchor in the tumultuous sea of their financial reality.

The figures weren't adding up the way they needed to. Each entry was a reminder of dreams so daringly chased and the precarious edge on which they now balanced. Lisa reached for the calculator, pressing the buttons with a determination born of necessity, but the stubborn math refused to yield more promising results.

It didn't look good.

A knot tightened in her stomach, an all-too-familiar guest whispering of looming challenges. They had come so far and worked tirelessly, yet the path ahead was shadowed with uncertainty. She let out a measured breath, trying to will away the anxiety that clawed at the edges of her resolve.

Outside, the world continued to turn, the café a living entity that thrummed with energy and life. But in the quiet sanctity of her office, Lisa Montgomery faced the daunting truth of their situation, armed with nothing but a ledger and the unwavering spirit that had carried her through storms before. If things didn't change, they'd have to close the café within six months.

The odds were against them.

⁂

The office's silence was punctuated by the soft clicks of the calculator, a metronome to Lisa's deepening frown. She didn't hear him approach, but she felt the change in the air as Oliver's presence filled the doorway.

"Hey," he said gently, his voice a balm to her fraying nerves. His hand found hers, rough from hours spent shaping wood, yet his touch was tender as it enveloped her smaller, work-worn fingers.

Lisa looked up, her eyes meeting his. There was an ocean of concern in his gaze, an echo of the sea he so missed.

"It'll be okay, Lisa," he said with a conviction that belied the fear she knew lived in his heart. "We've weathered worse."

She allowed herself a moment, just one, to lean into his strength. The familiar scent of sawdust and coffee on his shirt was grounding, a reminder of the life they were building together. Her shoulders, hunched in apprehension, relaxed incrementally under the weight of his reassurance.

"Thank you," she whispered, her voice barely above the hum of the refrigerator in the corner. She squeezed his hand, finding solace in their shared warmth and the silent promise that they were in this together. Yet she had never told him just how bad it actually was.

The sudden wail of their baby shattered the quiet, a piercing siren that spoke of hunger or perhaps a bad dream. Lisa's eyes closed briefly, the sigh escaping her lips carrying the weight of exhaustion. A night broken by cries and a morning filled with worry had taken its toll.

"I've got her," Oliver said before she could rise. He released Lisa's hand and strode toward the small cot tucked in the corner of the office. With practiced ease, he lifted Julia, cradling her against his chest as he murmured soothing words.

Lisa watched them; the sight was a fresh wave of love warming her chest. With his untamed hair and tired lines that had started to mark his face, Oliver was a portrait of paternal devotion. He caught her eye over the top of Julia's head and winked, a silent message of solidarity.

"Going for a walk," he mouthed, already wrapping Julia in her blanket. The stroller, always ready by the door, beckoned.

"Fresh air will do her good," Lisa called softly after them, her voice steady despite the chaos of her thoughts. She turned back to the ledger, the numbers still demanding her attention, but the edge of panic had dulled. The door chimed as Oliver left, the sound mingling with the fading cries of their youngest.

Alone again, Lisa drew a deep breath, the lingering touch of Oliver's hand a talisman against the tide of worries. They would make it through, somehow. They had to—for their family, for their dreams, for the love that bound them together against all odds.

The doorbell's gentle chime cut through the quiet hum of the cafe, a sound that usually heralded the comfort of routine. But as Lisa glanced up from the ledger's relentless figures, her pulse skipped erratically. The silhouette framed in the doorway wasn't one of their regulars; this was someone new, someone unexpected.

Sunlight glinted off delicate features and cascaded down a waterfall of dark hair, setting the woman aglow like some ethereal visitor. Beside her, a young boy clung to her hand, his wide eyes scanning the room with innocence. He was flicking curiously around the space, taking in the quaint ambiance of mismatched chairs and the smell of fresh coffee.

"Can I help you?" Lisa asked, tucking a stray wavy brown lock behind her ear, her voice steady despite the surprise of these unexpected visitors. Were they tourists?

The woman offered a tentative smile, drawing the boy closer to her side. "I'm looking for Oliver Thompson," she said, her voice resonant but carrying an undercurrent of nerves.

"Oliver's not here right now," Lisa replied, her heart beginning to thump erratically against her ribs. She could feel the weight of the woman's gaze, intense and searching. "Can I take a message?"

"Please," the woman hesitated, glancing down at the boy before locking eyes with Lisa again. "Tell him Ava was here. And Daniel. You know what? Do you mind if I wait? We've come a long way to see him."

Lisa felt the air grow still around her, the bustling sounds of the café receding into a distant hum as she pieced together the puzzle before her. She remembered Oliver's stories of a love lost, the woman who left him without a goodbye, without a reason. The same woman he had mourned the loss of, and that had made it hard for him to get involved again out of fear of abandonment once more. Now, they flashed through her mind, and here she was, the embodiment of his past, holding a child's hand.

"Of course," Lisa managed, her voice a touch softer than intended. "Why don't you come in and sit down? It might be a little while before he gets back."

Ava nodded, relief seeming to settle over her features as she ushered her son inside. Lisa watched the boy's hesitant steps, saw the way his gaze lingered on the wooden sailboats displayed on the shelves—Oliver's handiwork—and something protective welled up within her. This was their life, their sanctuary, and yet she couldn't ignore the tremor of uncertainty that whispered through her veins nor the compassion that urged her to extend kindness to this ghost from Oliver's past.

"Make yourselves comfortable," Lisa said, gesturing toward a cozy corner table. "Can I get you anything? Coffee? Tea? We have some freshly baked scones, too."

"Tea would be wonderful. Thank you," Ava said,

the tension easing from her shoulders as they sat down.

The boy looked up at Lisa with curiosity, and she gave him a reassuring smile, the same one she reserved for her own children when they were wary of new situations.

Lisa watched them settle in, her mind whirling with questions and what-ifs. The scent of wood shavings seemed to cling to the air, a reminder of Oliver's presence even in his absence. She thought of him out there, somewhere between the ocean he missed and the life they were trying to build together—a life that now felt as precarious as a ship caught in a sudden storm.

Lisa wiped her hands on her apron, the fabric a poor sponge for the clamminess of her palms. Every tick of the clock above the café door reverberated through the small space, marking the agonizing passage of time as she waited for Oliver. The low murmur of conversation from Ava and the boy was a distant hum in Lisa's ears, drowned out by the thumping of her heart.

She cast furtive glances at the pair, studying the boy's profile, and watched as Ava sipped at the tea she had accepted. Her demeanor was calm, but her eyes were holding stories yet untold.

Ava leaned against the polished wooden table, her hands casually wrapped around a warm mug, the steam curling like whispers into the air.

"I forgot how cold it gets here," she said, her voice as smooth as the tea in her cup, and Lisa couldn't help but notice how the morning light played with the edges of Ava's dark hair, lending her an ethereal quality.

"Yeah, it can get rough around here," she replied, matching Ava's smile with one of her own—a practiced gesture that reached her eyes more easily than she expected.

"I don't think this café was here when I was here last, but then again. It was also a lot of years ago," Ava said. "It's new? Someone told me Oliver started it up?"

"Yes, he and I started the Seabreeze Café together," Lisa said, trying to make sure the woman understood that they were a couple. Then she added: "He took our youngest for a small walk so she could nap. She's six months old. He'll be back soon. What brings you to our little corner of the world?"

"I guess I needed a change of scenery," Ava confessed, her gaze wandering toward the window where the ocean danced with the shore in an endless waltz. "There's something about the simplicity here, the way nature is so intertwined with life… It's captivating."

Lisa nodded, understanding the lure all too well—the same siren call of the waves had anchored her here. The rhythm of the rolling tide was like a steady heartbeat beneath the bustle of the café, grounding them both in the moment.

Lisa had used the same lie when she came here, using the phrase that she needed "a change of scenery" when, in reality, she was running from her past, an abusive husband—Ethan and Abigail's father.

Lisa knew Ava was lying, too. It was very obvious. And now she wondered what the woman really was doing here. And why was she asking for Oliver?

"Nature does have a way of casting its spell here," Lisa agreed, briefly snagging on the sight of Oliver's latest wood carving displayed on a nearby shelf. His craftsmanship was another echo of the town's raw beauty.

"How do you know Oliver?" Lisa asked, even though she already knew.

The name dropped between them like a stone into still water, sending ripples through Lisa's composure. Her heart hitched, the easy cadence of their conversation disrupted by a sudden surge of surprise.

A subtle shift in Ava's blue eyes suggested layers yet to be uncovered, but whatever lay behind those depths remained hidden for now. In the charged silence that followed, Lisa's thoughts tumbled over one another—curiosity, concern, and a protective instinct she wasn't fully aware she possessed until this very moment.

Ava's lips parted, then closed, as though deciding how much to divulge, and Lisa held her breath, waiting for answers that seemed as vast and deep as the ocean itself.

❧

Ava's fingers traced the rim of her teacup, a small gesture betraying an inner turmoil that belied her calm exterior. Lisa watched, a knot tightening in her stomach as the seconds stretched into a silence thick with unspoken words. The cadence of waves outside seemed to pause, waiting for Ava's revelation.

"Oliver," Ava began, her voice a soft wisp of sound that barely carried over the murmur of the cafe, "he's from my past." She met Lisa's gaze squarely, the determination in her eyes clashing with the vulnerability of her confession. "I need to talk to him."

The words hung in the air, each syllable laden with implications that sent Lisa's mind spinning with a jealousy she hadn't encountered before.

Lisa's heart thrummed in her chest, a staccato beat echoing the relentless crash of waves. She couldn't shake the image of Oliver on his old boat, the one he spoke of with a mix of longing and resignation. Had Ava stood beside him on that weathered deck, sharing the triumphs and trials of his past fisherman's life? Or was she the one waiting for him as he docked after a hard day's work, dreaming only of throwing himself into her warm embrace?

Lisa's thoughts tumbled and quickly became a cascade of doubts and fears. Her love for Oliver was a lighthouse in her life, guiding her through the fog of past hardships. The idea that Ava might be a link to a part of him she never knew—a part he never shared—sent a cold shiver down her spine.

Each possibility held its own form of suspense, a narrative thread that could unravel the tapestry of the life she had carefully woven with Oliver. Lisa's nurturing instincts warred with a protective urge, the latter a fierce flame fanned by the unknown elements of Ava's story.

"Did he ever mention me?" Ava's question broke through Lisa's reverie, pulling her back to the moment where questions demanded answers and the past threatened to collide with the future.

"Oliver keeps his cards close," Lisa replied, her voice steadier than she felt. She lied. Oliver had mentioned Ava on one occasion when they had talked about loves lost. She had offered him comfort, thinking—and hoping—they'd never see this woman again. The grief of the lost love visible in his eyes was one she never wanted to see again.

"But I'm sure he'll want to see you when he returns."

She offered a smile, though it didn't reach her eyes, which remained fixed on Ava, searching for clues in the subtlest twitch of her lips or the slightest flicker in her deep blue gaze.

As the two women waited there, the comforting scent of coffee mingling with the briny fragrance drifting in from the sea, the cafe's atmosphere shifted imperceptibly from serene to charged. Lisa's world, once defined by the rhythm of small-town life and the steady heartbeat of family, now teetered on the edge of a precipice, awaiting the return of the one man who could pull all the pieces into place—or scatter them to the winds.

Lisa could feel the weight of each second as it passed, the ticking of the cafe's old clock punctuated by Ava's soft breaths and the distant call of gulls outside. She studied the woman before her, the edges of her own thoughts frayed with concern and curiosity.

"Listen," Lisa began, her voice a blend of warmth and caution, "Oliver should be back soon, but you can also come back later if you're tired of waiting?"

"I don't mind waiting."

Ava's eyes, a striking shade of cobalt that seemed to mirror the ocean itself, met Lisa's with a mix of relief and apprehension.

"We can go upstairs to our living room if you prefer," Lisa said.

"Thank you. I appreciate you letting us wait here," she said, her smile fraught with unspoken tales.

As they entered the living room, its walls adorned with pictures of smiling faces and hand-crafted wooden frames—a testament to Oliver's craftsmanship—Daniel rushed ahead, his youthful energy a whirlwind in the serene space. The little boy, no more than five, with his tousled dark hair and bright eyes, immediately found solace in a toy car, which he zoomed across the hardwood floor with abandon. His laughter, pure and untainted by the complexities of adult emotions, echoed through the room, mingling with the soft crackle of the fireplace.

Lisa watched Daniel play, the tension in her shoulders easing slightly at the sight of his innocent joy. She motioned for Ava to take a seat on the plush sofa, its cushions worn in just the right places from years of use. A throw blanket, knitted in hues of blue and green, lay folded neatly on the backrest—a small, comforting detail in the midst of uncertainty.

"Make yourself at home," Lisa offered, her tone genuine despite the whirlpool of questions churning within her. She settled into an armchair adjacent to the sofa, her gaze wandering from Ava's contemplative expression to Daniel's animated play.

Outside, the shadows grew longer as the day waned, and inside, two women sat, each wrapped in their own thoughts, while a little boy played, blissfully unaware of the storm that might be brewing over the horizon.

Lisa rose gracefully from her seat and strode to the kitchen, the hem of her apron swaying with each step. She returned shortly, a plate of freshly baked cookies in hand, their sweet aroma wafting through the room. Daniel's eyes lit up at the sight, his toy car momentarily forgotten.

"Would you like a cookie, Daniel?" Lisa asked, her voice soft but laced with warmth as she crouched down to his level.

"Chocolate chip, my favorite!" he exclaimed, acccpting the treat with sticky fingers. His small teeth sank into the gooey center, a smile spreading across his face, chocolate smudges painting his cheeks.

"I bet you're quite the explorer," Lisa said, engaging him. Her heart swelled with an affection that seemed to come naturally around children.

"Uh-huh," Daniel nodded enthusiastically, crumbs tumbling from his lips. "I found a big rock today! It looked like a dinosaur egg!"

"Is that so?" Lisa chuckled. The innocence of youth was a balm to any troubled soul, she thought, watching his animated gestures.

"Mommy says we're gonna find lots of cool stuff here," he added with the certainty only a child could possess.

"Indeed, you will," Lisa assured him, brushing his hair back gently. She turned her attention back to Ava, who watched the exchange with a tender gaze, making Lisa's heart pound with curiosity over their shared connection to Oliver.

"Daniel seems to be liking it here," Lisa began, easing into the conversation. "And how about you, Ava?"

Ava took a deep breath, her hands clasped tightly as if gathering strength from the contact.

"It's… complicated," she finally admitted, her eyes darting away before locking back onto Lisa's. "You see, Oliver and I, we have history."

"History?" Lisa echoed, her pulse quickening. She felt as though she were standing on the edge of a revelation, the weight of the unknown pressing down on her.

"Oliver was my first love," Ava confessed, the words hanging between them like a delicate thread about to snap. "We were young, full of dreams and promises. But life… has a way of taking unexpected turns. I left Alaska, and it broke both our hearts."

Lisa absorbed every word, and the puzzle pieces slowly formed an image she hoped didn't exist anymore. The love in Ava's eyes when speaking of Oliver frightened her to the core. Her mind raced, trying to reconcile this piece of Oliver's past with the man she knew now.

"Then why return after all these years?" Lisa's question was gentle but loaded with the gravity of their situation.

"Because there are things left unsaid, and I need closure," Ava replied, her voice barely above a whisper. "And because… because Daniel deserves to know about his father."

The air seemed to still around them, the implication of Ava's words settling like dust after a storm. Lisa felt the ground shift beneath her, the mixture of heartwarming nostalgia and thrilling suspense leaving her on the precipice of an answer she wasn't sure she was ready to hear.

"Daniel is…."

"Oliver's son," Ava finished for her, her eyes reflecting a sea of emotions.

Lisa sat motionless, the only sound in the room the soft crunch of a cookie being devoured by an oblivious child, unaware of the depth of the conversation unfolding around him. The significance of what Ava had revealed coiled tight in Lisa's chest, anticipation and apprehension wound together in a dance as old as time itself.

Lisa's fingers curled tightly around the plate of cookies she was holding. Her heart throbbed against her ribcage—a drumbeat of dread and love playing a discordant melody. Ava's revelation hung between them, a specter of the past that now threatened to overshadow Lisa's present. The porcelain of the plate felt cool and fragile, much like the sense of stability she had cultivated with Oliver.

"Oliver and I—we've built something here," Lisa began, her voice a hesitant tremor. She searched Ava's face, seeking an understanding that would bridge the chasm of emotions yawning within her. "I love him, Ava. We're a family."

Ava nodded, her expression etched with empathy. "I know. And I never meant to disrupt your lives. But Daniel has questions, and I can't lie to him anymore."

The two women sat in silence, a tableau of tension and unspoken fears. Lisa could feel the pull of her love for Oliver, the desire to protect the life they'd stitched together from the windswept threads of their individual pasts. Yet, she couldn't deny the echo of sorrow in Ava's words, the right of a child to know his roots. It was a tangled web of loyalties and longings, each thread delicate and laden with consequence.

"Whatever happens," Lisa whispered, more to herself than to Ava, "we'll find a way through it." Her declaration was a lifeline cast into uncertain waters, promising buoyancy amidst the storm of emotions.

Just as the weight of their conversation settled into a quiet understanding, a sound sliced through the mounting tension: the back door creaked open downstairs, its well-worn hinges protesting softly. Footsteps, familiar and heavy with the day's toil, approached. Then came the voice that had soothed Lisa's fears and shared her laughter, calling out with casual affection, "Lisa? I'm back!"

The words were simple, but they carried the weight of impending revelation. Lisa's breath caught in her throat, her eyes darting to Ava, whose poised calm seemed to falter for just a moment. The air was thick with anticipation, the scent of sea salt and spruce mingling with the rawness of human emotion.

"Oliver," Lisa called out, the name both a beacon and a warning. Her heart skipped wildly, racing toward the inevitable collision of past and present, love and truth.

As Oliver's footsteps neared the top of the stairs, the chapter closed on the precipice of a moment that held the power to unravel or mend the tapestry of their lives.

OLIVER

Oliver's hand was still on the doorknob when the sight that greeted him rooted his feet to the floor. Ava stood in the middle of the living room, the midday sunlight painting her silhouette in a stark contrast of light and shadow. Her dark hair tumbled around her shoulders like a cascading waterfall, and those piercing eyes that he'd known would forever be etched in his memory were fixed on him with an intensity that sent a jolt through his system.

Time seemed to stutter. A million memories flashed before Oliver's eyes—salt air, tangled sheets, and laughter that filled the tiny cabin of his fishing boat. His heart pounded against his ribcage, a drumbeat out of sync with the world around him.

"Oliver?" It was Lisa's voice, but it sounded distant, as if from another room or another time.

Lisa, with her wavy brown hair that always smelled like vanilla and her hands that never stopped moving—cooking, cleaning, soothing—stood by the fireplace, a tentative smile on her face as she tried to bridge the chasm of silence. Her eyes flickered between him and Ava, the warmth there tinged with worry, the embodiment of hearth and home that had finally grounded him. She walked to him and grabbed baby Julia from his hands. Oliver's eyes never left those of Ava.

"Wh-what are you doing here?" Oliver's voice sounded foreign to his own ears, rough and tinged with the shock that constricted his throat. The question hung heavy in the room, echoing against the walls adorned with pictures of his life with Lisa and the children—a life that felt a million miles away in the presence of his past.

Lisa stepped forward, her movements deliberate and careful, as if walking through a minefield.

"She just arrived," Lisa explained, her voice a soothing balm against the sharp edges of the situation. "We thought it would be best to talk things through… together." Her eyes held his, searching for understanding, for the resilience he loved about her, the resilience that had seen them both through so many of life's storms.

The tension in the room coiled tighter, a living thing. Oliver could feel the weight of unspoken words pressing down upon them, threatening to shatter the fragile peace they had built. He glanced at Ava, then back to Lisa, feeling as though he stood at the precipice of a vast and unknown sea, the ground beneath him giving way to the tumultuous waters of uncertainty and old ghosts that refused to rest.

Ava's hands were unsteady, her knuckles whitening as they gripped the back of the couch. She drew a deep breath, her gaze flitting between Oliver and the wooden floorboards as if the right words were etched into the grain.

"Oliver," she started, her voice threaded with a tremor that betrayed her calm facade, "I didn't come here to cause trouble."

Oliver remained still, his body rooted in place while his heart hammered against his ribs like a drumbeat, amplifying the suspense choking the air.

"Then, why?" The question was barely above a whisper, but it carried all the weight of his bewildered emotions.

"I came..." Ava paused, her eyes lifting to meet his, oceans of blue swirling with hope and fear. "I came to reconnect. With you."

She swallowed hard, and her next words reshaped the world as he knew it.

"Daniel... he's your son."

The room spun on its axis, leaving Oliver grasping for stability. His mind became a maelstrom of memories and present realities, each vying for dominance. Daniel—the boy with messy dark hair and laughter that seemed to echo through the walls, suddenly cast in a new, life-altering light.

He could feel the life he had meticulously built with Lisa, the comforting warmth of their shared existence, now teetering on the brink. Yet there was also the ghost of his past, Ava, her image interwoven with recollections of salt-sprayed kisses and promises whispered beneath a canopy of stars. Her revelation sent a surge of thrill through him, a thrill that was swiftly suffocated by the grip of responsibility for the life he had chosen.

How could he reconcile these two halves of his soul—the fisherman longing for the open ocean and the woodworker who had carved out a new path? Oliver's breath hitched, his eyes flicking from Ava's expectant face to Lisa's silent plea. A romance lost to time and a thriller unfolding before him, his very existence the stage for a heartwarming yet harrowing act in the play of his life.

Lisa's fingers trembled imperceptibly as she smoothed the creases from the linen tablecloth, her movements betraying a facade of calm. The air was thick with unspoken words and unasked questions, each breath feeling heavier than the last. With her heart pounding against her ribcage like a caged bird desperate for escape, she turned to Ava and Daniel, her voice faltering ever so slightly as she spoke.

"Please, stay for lunch," Lisa insisted, the offer hanging in the room like a delicate truce. The smile she offered them was warm, but her eyes were a tumultuous sea of concern and confusion. "I can close the café early today, and I'll whip something together for all of us."

Ava gave a hesitant nod, holding Daniel close. They took their seats at the table, which suddenly felt too small for the magnitude of emotions it now contained. Lisa busied herself with cooking and soon served the steaming dishes of food, an aromatic distraction from the tension that clung to every surface of the living room.

Abigail and Ethan came out from their rooms. They sat in silence, their young faces etched with the innocent bewilderment of children who sense the shift in their world without understanding its cause. They picked at their food, exchanging furtive glances that asked questions their lips dared not utter.

Caught in the storm's eye between his past and present, Oliver found his gaze locked on Ava. It was as if the years had peeled away, revealing the raw edges of a wound he thought had healed long ago. His throat tightened, words bottlenecking behind the dam of his emotions, leaving him mute and adrift in his turmoil.

Lisa felt the weight of her own discomfort settle around her shoulders like a shawl woven from needles and thread. She wanted to reach out, to smooth over the jagged silence that filled the spaces between them. But her hands, which had moved with purpose moments ago, now lay still in her lap, uncertain and heavy.

The meal continued, a symphony of clinking cutlery and unsaid truths, each bite tasting of the unknown future that loomed over them.

Ava's fingers traced the rim of her water glass, the condensation cool against her skin. The silence hung heavy in the air, and each breath seemed to weave a tighter web of tension around the room. Her eyes, usually so commanding, now flickered with an uncertain light that danced between hope and trepidation. She drew a shaky breath, her chest rising as she prepared to unravel the past that had silently stitched itself into the fabric of the present. The food was gone, eaten, and the children left the table to go enjoy the rest of their day. Lisa was in the kitchen, doing dishes, and it was time to break the silence. They both knew it and feared it. Ava did the talking.

"Oliver," Ava began, her voice a soft murmur barely louder than the rustle of leaves outside the window, "there's so much you don't know, things I've held onto for so long."

The words tumbled out, hesitant at first, then gaining momentum as if breaking free from the reservoir of her heart. She recounted the days when their love was a living thing, vibrant and wild before fate cruelly snipped their threads from its tapestry.

"We were torn apart by circumstance, by decisions made in desperate times. I wanted to tell you that I was pregnant, but the fear…."

Her voice trailed off, leaving the echo of unspoken regrets hanging between them. "My father sent me away when he found out. He didn't want anyone to know I had become pregnant out of wedlock. You know how religious they are. He was ashamed, he said. I had humiliated him in front of the entire town. You would never want me, he said, and I believed him. He gave me money and told me to get as far away as possible. I was scared. I left and found a life somewhere else, in a small town down south, raised Daniel for years alone, and worked as a waitress. It was hard, and I constantly thought about you, wanting you to know. But as the years went on, it got harder and harder to come back."

Lisa, who had been silent in the kitchen, finally returned to the dining room. Her hands, which were clasped tightly, now visibly trembled as she placed them on the polished wood surface and leaned forward. Her voice, though steady, betrayed the underlying current of her frayed nerves.

"Ava," she said, locking eyes with the woman who held fragments of Oliver's past, "why now? Why come back into our lives and reveal this about Daniel?"

There was no accusation in her tone, at least none that was intended, only the plaintive search for understanding, the need to comprehend the sudden jolt that threatened to dismantle the life they had carefully built.

The question hovered in the room, a specter that demanded an answer. Ava's gaze shifted from Lisa to Oliver, then down to her son, whose innocent laughter had once filled her world with light. It was for him she had come—for him, she had braved the ghosts of what could have been. With every ounce of strength she had mustered to arrive at this moment, Ava knew that the truth, however tumultuous, had to surface to give her son the one thing she always wanted for him —wholeness.

Oliver's hand trembled imperceptibly as he reached for the water glass, its contents rippling like his unsettled thoughts. He set it down without a sip, the clink of glass on wood punctuating the silence. His gaze, drifting from Ava's tormented eyes to Lisa's expectant ones, caught a glimmer of the ocean in their depths— the ocean that he longed for, that mirrored the tumult within him.

"Lisa," Oliver began, his voice a curious blend of sorrow and an ache for days long past. "I'd be lying if I said I hadn't thought about her… about what might have been." The words hung heavy, charged with the gravity of unsaid confessions and roads untaken.

Lisa's chest tightened, her heart drumming against her ribs like a bird frantic to escape its cage. She watched the man she loved grappling with specters of a life interrupted, and the room seemed to shrink, walls closing in with the weight of unspoken fears. Her fingers brushed against the wooden table, seeking something solid in the maelstrom of doubt.

"Oliver," she said; her voice was barely louder than a whisper, yet it sliced through the tension like a knife. Her eyes, brimming with tears that threatened to spill over, fixed on him with an intensity borne of desperation and love. "Do you still love her?" The question was a living thing between them, sharp and fraught with the power to cleave her world in two. "Would you leave us—leave me?"

The air quivered with the magnitude of her inquiry, and for a moment, time seemed to stand still, waiting for Oliver to cast the die that would determine their fates. Oliver felt the weight of her stare, the silent plea etched into every line of her face, the face that had become his light through stormy weather.

He wanted to wrap her in an embrace and shield her from the tempest of emotions that raged like the sea he so missed, but the truth was a gale that could not be calmed by mere wishes or wants. Oliver knew his next words would be the anchor or the tempest, the salvation or the wrecking wave.

"Lisa," he finally uttered, every syllable laced with turmoil and tenderness, "I can't deny the past, nor can I ignore the love we've nurtured here, with you, with the kids."

His hand reached out, hovering over hers, yearning to bridge the distance, to reconnect amidst the chaos. "This life, our life, is where my loyalty lies."

Tears escaped Lisa's hold, tracing trails of fear, relief, and love down her cheeks. She watched Oliver, this man of wood and waves, struggling against the pull of a bygone tide while anchoring himself firmly to the shore they had built together. It was heart-warming and thrilling, suspenseful and terrifying—all at once.

As the evening sun dipped below the horizon, casting a golden glow through the curtains, the room held its breath, awaiting the next chapter in a tale as unpredictable as the sea itself.

Though the fear of losing him clung to her like a shadow, Lisa found something akin to hope flickering within her chest. His words were like lighthouse beams piercing through fog, guiding her back from the brink of despair.

"Oliver, I..." she began, but no further words came. Instead, her hand reached across the table, past the saltshaker and the half-empty glasses, to find Oliver's. Her fingers brushed against the roughness of his, a woodworker's hand, and then closed around it. It was a simple gesture, but in that touch was the recognition of all the battles they had fought side by side, of quiet evenings and whispered dreams, of resilience that only love could weave.

She held on, her grip both delicate and defiant, a silent promise amidst the chaos: *I'm here; I understand, and we'll weather this storm together.*

Oliver felt the tremble in Lisa's touch, a subtle yet profound assurance anchoring him more securely than any harbor could. In that contact, the electricity of unspoken words danced between them—a dance of trust, shared scars, and love that refused to be undone by the tempests of life.

Their joined hands became the focal point in the room, a symbol of unity that faced down the specter of their complicated past. Oliver's eyes met Lisa's, finding there not just forgiveness but a recognition of their journey, a testament to the love that had grown, weathered, and blossomed in the fertile soil of their togetherness.

And so, they remained with his hand in hers, bonded by an understanding deeper than the ocean he longed for, stronger than the finest wood he had ever shaped.

Ava caught the silent exchange between Oliver and Lisa, the entwining of hands that spoke volumes in the quiet room. She exhaled slowly, a breath she hadn't realized she'd been holding, as the realization settled over her like the softest shroud. Her gaze, once locked onto Oliver with a fierce hope, softened at its edges, now tinged with the gentle hue of resignation.

"Daniel needs stability," she murmured, more to herself than to the couple before her. Her voice, laced with the weight of her decision, filled the space between them—a space that had grown vast and insurmountable. With each word Ava spoke, she weaved the fabric of her son's future, choosing threads of security and happiness over the tangled yarns of what-ifs and might-have-beens.

She looked down at Daniel, his innocent eyes wide, reflecting the flickering candlelight on the dining table. His small hand found hers, his trust in her as boundless as the ocean.

It was for this boy, this beautiful culmination of

her past love and present strength, that she would lay down her own heartache.

"Oliver," Ava finally said, her voice steady despite the storm raging within her, "I want what's best for him. I want him to get to know you, his dad. Can we do that?"

At that moment, she was the epitome of maternal protection, her resolve as unyielding as the wood beneath Oliver's skilled hands—wood that could weather any storm when treated with care and purpose.

The room fell into a tense silence, heavy with the gravity of their intertwined lives. Lisa's hand remained steadfast in Oliver's, their fingers a testament to enduring love amidst the tempest of emotions that threatened to engulf them all.

Oliver's eyes roved from Lisa to Ava, and the internal struggle was clear on his face. Each thought, each fleeting emotion, etched deeper lines into his visage—the charming smile he once wore with ease was now a distant memory. He grappled with the pull of the past and the anchor of his present, his heart torn by the swell of conflicting tides.

With her eyes a well of empathy, Lisa watched the scene unfold, her heart thrumming with a cocktail of emotions—love, fear, and determination. The tremble in her touch had steadied, replaced by a resolve as unshakeable as the foundations of the home they had built together.

"Of course you can," Lisa answered for him. "The boy needs his father. You should be that to him."

Chapter Four

Lisa Montgomery sat at the desk, a fortress of paperwork and bills hemming her in on all sides. Her fingers traced the edges of an envelope, the motion mechanical, as if she could divine its contents through touch alone. With each crease and crumple under her fingertips, Lisa's brow furrowed deeper, a physical testament to the tumult of worry gnawing at her insides. No matter which way she spun them, the numbers still didn't add up, and a shiver of dread danced down her spine.

"Oliver," she whispered to the empty room, his name tasting like a plea on her lips. Their love was a lighthouse in the storm, but even lighthouses could falter against relentless waves. Could their relationship withstand the mounting pressures, or would it crumble like sandcastles to the tide? The numbers weren't good; they were actually very, very bad. And Oliver had gone fishing for the day on the river. It was Sunday, and the café was closed.

The front door creaked open, slicing through the silence. Sunlight poured into the room like liquid gold, heralding the arrival of Maggie Martin. Her curly red hair caught the light, setting it ablaze with fiery hues that defied the gloom of Lisa's thoughts. Maggie's smile was a warm blanket, wrapping around Lisa without a single word spoken.

"Hey there, stranger," Maggie chimed, her voice carrying the comforting familiarity of home. She closed the door behind her, the soft click resounding like a promise: You're not alone.

Lisa looked up, attempting to mask her turmoil with a thin veneer of composure. But Maggie knew her too well and saw right through the façade as easily as glass. There was no hiding from Maggie Martin, a truth Lisa found both terrifying and utterly heart-warming.

"Hey, Maggie," Lisa replied, her voice a thread-bare quilt, warmth fraying at the edges. "Just trying to make sense of all this." She gestured limply at the financial quagmire spread out before her, each document a wave threatening to pull her under.

Maggie walked over, her every step exuding the quiet confidence of a woman who had weathered her own storms. She pulled out a chair, the scrape against the floor a grounding note amidst the cacophony of Lisa's fears.

"Mind if I take a look?" Maggie asked, the offer hanging between them like a lifeline. Her eyes, bright with empathy and resolve, locked onto Lisa's, and for a moment, the weight of the world seemed a little less crushing.

❦

Maggie settled into the chair beside Lisa, their shoulders nearly touching in the cramped space.

"Talk to me," Maggie urged gently, her hand finding its way to Lisa's arm, a tactile whisper of support. Her fingers were warm, a subtle anchor in the storm of Lisa's emotions.

Lisa turned to face her, and the deep furrows in her brow softened just slightly. "It's like I'm caught in this riptide, Maggie," she confessed, her gaze flickering down to where Maggie's hand lay reassuring against her skin. "And every time I think I'm swimming back to shore, something pulls me right back out again."

Maggie's eyes reflected a pool of understanding, her head tilting in a silent nudge for Lisa to continue. She had been there before, treading water in life's tempests, and that shared history of hardship wove the tight bond between them.

"I remember a few years ago when the tavern nearly went under," Maggie began, her voice steady despite the tremor of past fears. "I was so close to giving up and letting it all go. But I learned something important—waves keep coming, but you learn how to ride them. You're one of the strongest swimmers I know, Lisa."

A small, tentative smile played at the edges of Lisa's lips, the first genuine sign of warmth since

Maggie had entered. Hearing someone else's story of survival was visceral comfort, a reminder that neither of them was navigating these waters alone.

"I'm sure your strength got you through then, Mags," Lisa murmured, leaning in closer now, a silent acknowledgment of the bond they shared. "But what if my strength isn't enough?"

"Then you lean on mine," Maggie said without hesitation, her grip tightening ever so slightly, a lifeline cast in the shape of friendship. "You lean on Oliver's, too. We're a lighthouse collective here, each of us beaming out to guide the others home. Things will change. I'm sure they will. Business will pick up, and soon, you'll see the numbers change. It's always tough in the beginning. That's why so few people start up their own business. If it were easy, everyone would do it."

"True," Lisa said, feeling encouraged.

"You can do it. I know you can," Maggie added. "Heck, if I can, it can't be that hard, right? You just gotta stick to your guns and keep at it."

She said it with hoarse laughter that cheered Lisa up even more.

Lisa's fingers drummed a staccato rhythm on the wooden table, her gaze drifting from the clutter of bills to the woman beside her. Maggie's eyes, a reflection of the fiery spirit within, held steadfastly to Lisa's with an almost palpable intensity.

"Lisa, look at me," Maggie's voice was firm yet threaded with warmth. "You've weathered worse storms than this, haven't you? You're not just surviving; you're building something beautiful here for you and those kids."

Lisa's breath hitched as she absorbed the weight of Maggie's words. "But sometimes, I feel like I'm building on sand, Mags. What if it all just… washes away?"

"Then you rebuild," Maggie replied, her tone unwavering. On rock this time, with Oliver. You have more strength in your little finger than most have in their whole body. Look at how far you've come. But even the strongest among us need to reach out sometimes."

A tremor ran through Lisa's frame, the idea of reaching out mingling with a rising tide of fear. She hadn't told Oliver just how bad things really were— she didn't want to worry him.

"I want to," she confessed, her voice thinning to a whisper. "But what if Oliver can't handle it? What if my worries push him away? I can't… I don't want to be a burden to him."

"Oliver loves you, Lisa. He chose this—chose you —with all that comes with it." Maggie's hand squeezed Lisa's, a lifeline in the uncertainty. "You won't know until you speak up. Trust isn't just about believing he'll stay; it's also about believing he wants to share the load."

Lisa's heart fluttered against her ribcage, the suspense of the unknown stretching out before her. In a way, it was thrilling to stand at the precipice of reve-lation, but the thrill was laced with an undercurrent of fear. Could she take that leap? Did she dare?

"Being vulnerable isn't the same as being weak, you know," Maggie continued. "It's throwing open the doors and letting someone see the real you, the one who struggles, fears, and needs. That's where the real connection happens, Lisa. That's where love grows."

The conversation ebbed and flowed, a dance of words and silences that spoke volumes. Through it all, Maggie remained steadfast, her presence a testament to the enduring power of connection and the unwavering belief in Lisa's ability to brave any storm.

As they spoke, the outline of a plan began to form; *how about if they did woodworking classes?* Maggie asked. Oliver could teach. Lots of people would come for that. Lisa's smile brightened. That was a great idea. People were always mesmerized by the things he created. Oliver was very talented. They always said they wished they could do that and wanted to learn how to do something like that.

"I'll start putting a class schedule together right away. And then I'll start advertising," Lisa said. "In the local paper, our webpage, and Facebook and Instagram. Maybe I can put some flyers up at your bar?"

"I don't see why not," Maggie said. "We're here to help each other."

With another deep, steadying breath, Lisa felt a swell of determination crest within her. Her gaze met Maggie's, and with a tremulous smile, she reached out, enveloping Maggie's hand with her own.

"Thank you, Maggie," Lisa murmured, her voice thick with gratitude. "Thank you for reminding me of who I am and for being here. Your friendship… it means more than I can say."

Maggie's smile was warm, a mirror of the affection and solidarity that had become the bedrock of their bond. "Always, Lisa. I'm always here for you."

As Lisa withdrew her hand, she straightened her shoulders, a newfound resolve sparking in her hazel eyes. It was thrilling to imagine a future where she didn't have to shoulder her burdens alone and could share every part of her journey with Oliver. And with Maggie's guidance, she felt ready to step into that possibility, to embrace the love and support waiting for her just beyond the veil of her own vulnerability.

As Lisa sat on the weathered wooden bench, the soft susurration of waves against the shore provided a tranquil soundtrack. The salty air mingled with the scent of seaweed and brine, grounding her in the moment. Her eyes lingered on the horizon, watching the tumultuous dance of the ocean, its surface reflecting the chaos in her own heart.

She pulled the stroller closer, a protective gesture, and brushed a strand of hair from Julia's peaceful face. The baby's serene expression offered silent encouragement, reminding Lisa of the life she and Oliver had created together, a symbol of their intertwined destinies.

Every crash of the waves seemed to echo the racing thoughts in Lisa's head. Would Oliver understand her fears, or would he see them as an insurmountable barrier? The suspense of waiting gnawed at her resolve, yet the sight of the expanse before her bolstered her courage. This was Oliver's refuge, the place he missed when he left the fisherman's life behind. Here, amid the timeless rhythm of the tides, they could find common ground.

A seagull's cry punctuated the air, lifting above the sound of the waves—a reminder that nature held both chaos and harmony. As the breeze teased tendrils of wavy brown hair around her face, Lisa drew in a breath laced with briny moisture and closed her eyes. She envisioned the conversation to come, one that would lay bare her soul. It was a risk, but one she knew she must take if she wanted to build a future where honesty and love coexisted.

Her phone, silent until now, vibrated softly against her thigh. Heart leaping, she reached for it, her pulse quickening with a mix of dread and anticipation. It was time. Oliver's reply was brief but filled with promise; he and Mark had just returned from fishing, and she had asked him to meet her at their favorite spot by the ocean.

He wrote: "On my way."

She tucked the phone away, steeling herself for the moment of truth. Oliver would be here soon, and with him, the chance to strengthen the fragile bonds of their shared dreams. Today, the ocean wasn't just a soothing presence; it was a witness to the thresholds they were about to cross together.

The crunch of gravel underfoot announced his arrival before she saw him. Lisa's heart skipped as she turned, her gaze locking onto Oliver's form striding toward her. The late afternoon sun caught in the untamed waves of his dark hair, casting a halo of light that seemed to follow him. His eyes, a clear blue reminiscent of the sea before them, found hers, and in an instant, the world narrowed down to the space between them.

"Hey," he called out, his voice carrying over the sound of the surf, tinged with that familiar warmth that always seemed to wrap around her like a comforting shawl.

"Oliver," she breathed, rising from the bench as he closed the distance with a few long strides. His smile, broad and genuine, was a light that drew her in, chasing away the shadows that had gathered in the corners of her mind.

He knelt before Julia and tickled her stomach. "How's my girl doing?"

Then he hugged Lisa. Oliver's arms were strong but gentle, enveloping her in a sense of safety only he could provide. She felt the steady beat of his heart against her chest, a rhythm as reassuring as the ocean's pulse.

Pulling back slightly, Lisa searched his face, finding nothing but open affection there. It fortified her resolve.

"I need to talk to you," she said, the words coming

out in a rush. Her hands fidgeted with the hem of her shirt, betraying her inner turmoil.

"Okay, " Oliver's thumbs brushed soothing circles on her back. "What's going on?"

She hesitated, her mouth dry. This was the moment. "I'm scared," she confessed, the admission feeling like a crack in a dam holding back a torrential flood. "Scared that everything we're building is going to come crashing down around us… and that I'll be the reason for it."

Oliver's brow furrowed with concern, and he leaned back to look at her, his hands resting on her shoulders. "Lisa, talk to me. What's brought this on?"

"It's just…" She swallowed hard, gathering the fragments of her courage. "The bills, the business, Julia… Sometimes, I feel like I'm one step away from drowning, and I don't want to pull you down with me."

"Hey, hey…" He cradled her face in his hands, his touch grounding. "You're not alone in this. We're in it together, remember? There's no way you could ever be a burden to me."

Tears welled in her eyes, held at bay by the intensity of his gaze—a mirror reflecting back her own fears and hopes. "But what if—"

"No 'what ifs,'" he interrupted softly. "We'll tackle each day as it comes—you, me, and the kids. That's what families do. We hold each other up."

"But it's worse than I've told you. A lot worse. If we don't turn the business around in six months, we'll have to close it."

He nodded as if mulling over the news for a second. His silence brought great fear to Lisa. Would he give up on her?

"We'll figure something out," he said.

"I might have an idea. Actually, it was Maggie's, but I thought it might work."

"And what is that?" Oliver asked.

"We start wood carving classes, or rather you do, since you'd be teaching them. How does that sound?" she asked nervously.

Oliver went pale. "Teaching? I… I don't think that's something I'd be very good at. I'm not sure about that, Lisa."

She swallowed, feeling the weight of the situation on her shoulders. "But we have to do something, Oliver. We have to turn this business around, or we'll lose everything."

"I could always go back to being a fisherman," he said.

"But the children and I would never see you, and what about our dream? What about the café?"

He pulled her close and held her tight. "Shh, don't worry, sweetie. We'll come up with something. We'll solve this."

She nodded, feeling heavy and tired. "Maybe we could spend the day together tomorrow? Try and come up with a plan? Do some brainstorming?"

He made a weird face. "Ugh, tomorrow is no good."

"Why not?"

"I promised I'd spend time with Daniel, you know, get some father-son bonding."

She exhaled deeply, then nodded. "Yes, yes, of course."

He planted a kiss on her forehead. It made her feel like a child. "You're the best, do you know that?"

"I do," she mumbled, then got up from the bench and grabbed the stroller. Oliver put a hand on her back, a gentle, comforting movement that failed to make her forget her worry. If Oliver was spending time with Daniel tomorrow, that meant he was seeing Ava, too.

Chapter Five

The first rays of dawn had barely grazed the horizon when Lisa's eyes fluttered open. She lay still for a moment, the soft breathing of her children in adjacent rooms a comforting lullaby. But with each breath, her resolve strengthened—today, she would be the beacon of stability and warmth her family needed.

With gentle movements, Lisa slipped from beneath the covers, her feet landing softly on the cool wooden floor. She tiptoed to the kitchen, where the ritual of breakfast preparation awaited her. The clink of porcelain plates being set on the table, the sizzle of eggs in the skillet, and the aroma of toasted bread filled the space with an inviting atmosphere that spoke of normalcy and love.

"Morning, Mom," Ethan mumbled as he shuffled into the kitchen, his green eyes still heavy with sleep.

"Good morning, sweetheart," Lisa greeted him with a smile that didn't quite reach her eyes, her mind replaying Oliver's words from the day before—he would spend the day with Ava and young Daniel. It was important; she knew that, but it still left a hollow feeling in her chest.

"Is that bacon I smell?" Abigail chimed in, her curly hair bouncing as she skipped toward the scent.

"Of course," Lisa replied, channeling all her affection into her voice. "And I've made your favorite pancakes, too."

As they gathered at the table, Lisa's gaze lingered on baby Julia, peacefully sitting in the high chair, tapping a plastic spoon rhythmically against the table. This was her family, her world, and she'd protect their joy at all costs. The children laughed and chatted about the day ahead, and for a fleeting moment, the specter of Ava's return receded into the shadows.

The school run was always a bustling affair, with children streaming into the building with backpacks bouncing and parents exchanging hurried goodbyes. As Lisa maneuvered through the throng with Julia snuggled against her chest, subtle murmurs from other moms began to weave their way into her consciousness.

"Did you hear that Ava is back?"

"Yes, poor Lisa. We all remember how heartbroken Oliver was when Ava left. It can't be easy…."

Lisa's steps faltered for a heartbeat, the whispers clawing at her composure. She could feel the prying eyes, the unspoken pity, and the thirst for gossip. But no, she wouldn't let them see her waver. For Ethan and Abigail, who waved goodbye with innocent smiles, she had to be a fortress.

"Come on, Jules," she whispered to the baby, who gurgled obliviously, "let's get away from all this noise."

Head held high, Lisa strode from the school grounds, the murmurings fading behind her like an unsettling breeze. She felt the thrill of the challenge ahead, paired with the suspense of unknown outcomes. Yet, in her heart, there was a steady beat of determination; she would face whatever came with grace and resolve. After all, she was Lisa Montgomery, and she was made of sterner stuff.

The bell above the cafe door chimed a familiar, comforting note as Lisa pushed it open. A whiff of freshly ground coffee beans and the buzz of early customers waiting outside greeted her, wrapping around her senses like a welcome embrace. Yet beneath the layers of warmth and roasted aromas, the tendrils of stress crept in, coiling around her resolve.

"Steady, Lisa," she murmured to herself, rolling back her shoulders as she stepped behind the counter after putting Julia down for her nap. The scent of pine from the adjoining woodwork shop mingled with the coffee, grounding her. Her hands were steady as they flipped the sign to "Open."

Today, like every day, she would keep the heart of her business beating strong.

Orders flowed in like a relentless stream, and Lisa became a conductor orchestrating an intricate symphony of tasks. She shuttled between the espresso machine's hiss and the cash register's chime, all while keeping a watchful eye on the woodworking shop through the internal window that bridged the two worlds she had created.

"Morning, Lisa!" called out a regular, his voice cutting through the hum of activity. "I'll have the usual, and oh—is that new cedar piece ready?"

"Give me just a sec, Frank," she replied, her voice the epitome of small-town warmth yet edged with the sharpness of someone who knew how to get things done. She swiftly keyed in his order before slipping through to the back, where the scent of sawdust was thick, and promises were carved into reality.

Her fingers traced over the smooth surface of Frank's custom-ordered cedar shelf, ensuring perfection. Oliver had finished it late the night before so he could take off and be with his son. It was beautiful. Oliver really was the best at what he did.

Returning to the café, she placed the wrapped shelf on the counter with a triumphant smile. She exchanged pleasantries but never allowed the conversation to distract her from the next customer waiting patiently in line.

"Lisa, we're running low on the Guatemala blend," Marianne, her young half-time employee, called out, a hint of urgency threading her voice.

"Got it covered," Lisa assured, her response swift as she pivoted to the storeroom. Inventory lists danced in her head, a mental checklist that she ticked off with each step. The shelves were lined with neatly labeled bins, and she quickly located the needed coffee, restocking with efficient grace.

As the sun arced higher, casting beams of light through the café's front windows, Lisa's pace remained unyielding. She poured lattes with precision, frothing milk into creamy peaks while her mind orchestrated the inventory dance behind the scenes. The sweet aroma of pastries mixed with the tang of varnish was an olfactory reminder of the dual nature of her work.

The thrill of the challenge kept her alert, and the suspense of what lay beyond each brewed pot or sanded edge kept her engaged. There was no room for doubt—no space for the whispers that tried to seep in from the outside world.

"Keep pushing forward," she whispered to herself, a mantra that carried her through the day. Deep down, she knew that the foundation she laid with every cup served and every board smoothed was not just for the business but for the family she cherished beyond measure.

The bell above the cafe door chimed its familiar tone, signaling another customer had stepped into the warm embrace of Lisa's crafted world. Amidst the hum of conversation and the clinking of cups, she caught Marianne's eye from across the counter. The young waitress was wrestling with the espresso machine, her forehead creased in concentration. With a reassuring smile, Lisa made her way over, her hands expertly adjusting the dials as she guided Marianne's efforts.

"Remember, it's all about finding the right pressure," Lisa said, her voice an anchor amid the frothing steam.

Marianne nodded, her smile blooming as the coffee poured in a perfect, honey-colored stream.

"Thanks, Lisa."

It wasn't just about serving food and drinks but about fostering a team, a family almost, within the wooden walls that held their dreams. Each interaction, each shared victory with her staff, rekindled the fire in Lisa's chest, warming her against the chill of uncertainty that lingered just outside her reach.

A lull between orders granted Lisa a moment of respite. She retreated to the small office at the back, a sanctuary of paperwork and plans. No sooner had she taken a seat when her phone vibrated insistently against the desk. Oliver's name flashed on the screen, sending a jolt through her heart.

"Hey," she answered, bracing herself for whatever news might follow.

"Lisa, hi. We're doing okay here," Oliver's voice came through, tinged with an optimism she wished she could fully share. "Daniel is quite the character; he's got this laugh that's… well, it's something else."

She pictured Oliver's face, the way his eyes softened when joy touched his lips, and allowed herself a half-smile.

"I'm glad to hear that. How's Ava?" She regretted the question as soon as it left her lips.

"She's fine," he replied with a chuckle that sounded almost like affection—she could hear it. "We're slowly making headway. It's a lot to process for all of us."

She wanted to ask what kind of headway and what was a lot to process. Your love for Ava? Are your feelings coming back?

But she didn't. Of course not.

"Take your time, Ollie. You're doing great," Lisa encouraged, the words steady though her insides churned with a cocktail of emotions. Her support was unwavering, even if it meant navigating the stormy waters of the unknown.

"Thanks, Lisa. I'll be home after I drop them off at the inn. We'll talk more then?" The question hung in the air, an invisible thread connecting them.

"Of course. See you tonight," she said, the call ending with a click that resonated louder than she expected.

Lisa sat for a moment longer, her thoughts swirling like the leaves outside the window caught in an autumn gust. But the café beckoned her back, its pulse alive with the day's rhythm. With a deep breath, she stood, smoothing the front of her apron.

"Let's keep moving," she whispered to herself, the mantra a silent echo of the one that had carried her through the morning.

The pulse of excitement for what she had built never waned, nor did the thrill of the unknown that awaited her. It was a delicate dance along the edge of suspense, each step forward a testament to the heartwarming life she was determined to cultivate and defend.

&

Lisa's fingers danced across the cash register, the familiar melody of buttons and beeps playing along with the hum of conversation filling the cafe. A steaming mug of coffee clutched in her hand offered a momentary respite from the endless list of tasks. With each sip, she felt the warmth seep through her, but it did little to still the fluttering in her stomach—the constant reminder of Oliver's call.

We're making headway. It's a lot to process.
Ugh.

The chime above the door signaled another customer's entrance, snapping Lisa back into the present. She greeted them with her practiced smile, the one that said all was well in her world even when doubt shadowed her heart. The whispers about Oliver and Ava had been like tiny thorns in her side since morning, and as the sun traced its arc across the sky, the shadows grew longer, as did her contemplation of their past.

We all remember how heartbroken Oliver was.

"Is he still in love with her? Can they step back into old rhythms? And where does that leave us?" she mused silently while refilling the sugar containers. Her love for Oliver was like the woodwork adorning the café, carved deeply and with care, yet now she feared it might splinter under the strain of secrets long buried, of longings never met.

"Mom!" The voice of her son, Ethan, yanked her from her thoughts. He stood there with Abigail, their faces flushed from the brisk walk home from school.

"Hey, you two! How was school today?" Lisa bent down to wrap them both in a hug, feeling the tension ease just slightly at their touch. Their innocence was her balm, their presence her anchor.

"Good! But…" Ethan hesitated, his green eyes searching Lisa's. "Is it true about Oliver and… Ava?"

Abigail's small hand found Lisa's, her curious gaze mirroring her brother's concern.

Lisa straightened, steadying herself against the counter. "There are things from the past that are complicated, sweetie," she admitted, tucking a loose curl behind Abigail's ear. "But what matters is that we're a family. No matter what happens, we stick together."

"Is Daniel going to be our brother now?" Abigail asked, her voice a mix of hope and confusion.

"Let's take it one day at a time." Lisa bent down, bringing herself eye-to-eye with her children. "Right now, let's focus on being friends with them, okay? Welcoming them to the town. Families come in all shapes and sizes, but the love we have is what makes us strong."

Ethan nodded, a serious expression crossing his youthful face as he accepted the weight of his mother's words. Abigail smiled, squeezing Lisa's hand tighter as if to reinforce the bond between them.

"Can we help around the shop?" Ethan offered, and Lisa's heart swelled with pride.

"Of course," she said, grateful for the distraction. "You can start by helping me restock the napkin holders."

"Yay, I want to help too!" Abigail cheered, her enthusiasm momentarily dispelling the clouds of uncertainty.

Together, they turned toward the task, Lisa's determination reignited by the simple joy of her children's willingness to stand with her. Each fold of a napkin and each placement of a cup became an act of defiance against the whispers and worries trying to split them apart.

"Thank you, guys. You're my little heroes," Lisa whispered, watching them work with earnest dedication. In this small town where secrets whispered like wind through the trees, she'd keep the flame of her family's unity burning bright.

The aroma of rosemary and roasted chicken filled the cozy kitchen as Lisa, with practiced grace, shuffled between the stove and the countertop. She hummed softly to herself, a tune her mother used to sing when she was a child, as she stirred the simmering pot of homemade gravy. The golden light of early evening poured through the window, casting a warm glow over the dinner table she had meticulously set with their best china. In each detail—the folded napkins, the carefully placed cutlery, the vase of freshly picked wildflowers—Lisa wove a tapestry of comfort, aiming to cocoon her family from the storms outside.

Her movements were fluid, almost dance-like, as she added a pinch of salt here and a dash of pepper there while keeping a watchful eye on baby Julia, who gurgled happily. Ethan and Abigail, now engrossed in their homework at the kitchen island, occasionally looked up to sneak peeks at their mother, telling her they were hungry and asking when the food would be done.

The door creaked open, and Oliver stepped inside, the cool evening breeze slipping in behind him. He paused momentarily, taking in the scene before him: the children at ease, the baby's infectious laughter, the sumptuous spread on the table. His eyes met Lisa's, and time seemed to stand still for that fleeting second. Her smile was the light he had sought so often these past days, yet beneath it, he sensed the undercurrent of worry that threatened to pull her under.

"Smells amazing in here," Oliver said, his voice threading through the air like the delicate strains of Lisa's humming. He leaned down to plant a soft kiss on baby Julia's forehead, eliciting a squeal of delight from the little one.

"Thanks," Lisa replied, turning her attention back to the gravy boat in her hands. "I thought we could use a nice family dinner tonight."

Oliver nodded, running a hand through his tousled dark hair—a habit that betrayed his efforts to hide his unease. As he hung up his jacket, he glanced at the table setting, the effort Lisa had put into it a silent testament to her determination to maintain normalcy. He wanted to say more, to peel away the layers of tension that had settled between them, but the words felt heavy on his tongue.

"Can I help with anything?" he offered instead, reaching for the salad tongs.

"No, it's all under control. Why don't you sit down and relax for a bit? Dinner will be ready soon." Her voice was gentle, yet there was a firmness, a subtle armor she wore to defend against the uncertainty gnawing at her heart.

Oliver pulled out a chair but remained on his feet, leaning against it as he watched Lisa glide around the kitchen. There was something mesmerizing about her resilience, the way she held herself amid the whirlwind of emotions they both knew swirled around them.

"Hey, Oliver!" Ethan called out, breaking the spell. "Can you help me with a math problem? I'm not sure I got it right."

"Let me see, buddy," Oliver said, smiling as he walked over to inspect the homework. He ruffled Ethan's hair affectionately, a surge of pride mingling with an unspoken fear of the unknown. "You nailed it. It's perfect."

Lisa observed them from the corner of her eye, allowing herself a momentary respite from her inner turmoil. Whatever tomorrow might bring, she thought, they would face it together—as a family. With a final stir of the gravy, she announced, "Dinner's ready," and the comforting clatter of dishes and cutlery began, a symphony of domesticity that, for now, held the night's shadows at bay.

❧

The last of the dinner plates had been cleared away, the children's laughter now just an echo in the dimly lit kitchen. Lisa watched through the window as the sun dipped below the mountains, painting the sky with streaks of orange and purple. She clutched the hem of her apron, feeling the fabric's weave beneath her fingers.

"Lisa?" Oliver's voice was soft and tentative as he stepped into the room, his shadow stretching across the floorboards.

"Julia's finally asleep," she said, turning toward him, her expression a careful blend of affection and weariness.

"Good, good." He ran a hand through his hair, dark strands standing rebelliously against his palm. "We need to talk."

She nodded, bracing herself for the conversation she knew they couldn't avoid any longer. They moved to the living room, a space that felt too vast for just the two of them. Settling on the couch, their bodies were close, but their spirits were miles apart.

"Oliver, I—" Lisa began, but her words tangled like knotted wood shavings in her throat.

"Lisa, I know this is hard. I never meant for Ava's return to—"

"Upend our lives?" Lisa interjected, the hurt

61

spilling over. "You've been so distant since she arrived, and I don't know where we stand anymore."

Oliver reached for her hand, his fingers rough from crafting wood yet gentle in their touch. "I love you. And the kids. That hasn't changed. But Daniel…." His voice trailed off.

"Is he going to be part of our family now?" Lisa's question hung between them, fraught with implications.

"Daniel is my son. I want to be there for him, but not at the expense of what we've built." Oliver's eyes searched hers, seeking an anchor in the tumult.

"Can we even afford this? The shop, the café—they're barely breaking even. Now, with Ava and Daniel…." Lisa's resolve wavered as she pictured the precarious balance of their finances teetering on the edge.

"Hey, we'll figure it out. We always do." Oliver's assurance felt hollow, and his smile didn't quite reach his eyes.

"Always do?" Lisa's voice rose, sharpened by fear and frustration. "What if we can't?"

"Then what are you saying, Lisa?" Oliver's temper flared, mirroring her own. "That we just give up?"

"Of course not!" The words erupted from her, charged with all the love and determination she held for her family. "But we need to be realistic about—"

A sharp cry pierced through their argument, Julia's wails sounding from the nursery. Lisa stood abruptly, the maternal instinct trumping all else. As she hurried to comfort her baby, the tension with

Oliver remained unresolved, a heavy fog settling over the house.

Later that night, after Julia had been soothed back to sleep with whispered lullabies and tender caresses, Lisa found herself alone in the small office downstairs. The day's receipts lay uncounted, abandoned in favor of staring blankly at the moonlit patterns dancing on the wall. Exhaustion tugged at the edges of her consciousness, but her mind refused to still, replaying the argument, the fears, and the unspoken words.

Above her, in the bedroom, Oliver lay in bed alone. His thoughts churned like storm-tossed waters, filled with love for Lisa and the life they had started to build, yet tormented by the unforeseen riptides of Ava's return. For many years, he had wished—and prayed—she would return to him. And now, she had. His feelings for her were still there, undeniably. But he also loved Lisa, and especially the family they had built. But today, when Ava had taken his hand in hers while watching Daniel on the playground, he had felt a surge of emotions rush through him. All the old feelings that had been lurking beneath the surface came back. He still loved her. He had to admit to it. But was it enough to want to upend his life? His family?

He closed his eyes, willing sleep to come, but found himself adrift in the uncertainty of their future.

As the clock ticked steadily onward, marking the passage of time in the silent house, Lisa and Oliver each faced their own restless battles. Despite the distance that had crept into their bed, they shared a common hope—a guiding light in the darkness—that somehow, they would find a way to navigate through this… together.

&a;

Lisa rose from the creaky chair in her office, the moonlight casting a silver sheen on her wavy brown hair. She wrapped her cardigan tighter around her slender frame, feeling the cool night air that seeped through the old window frames. Moving silently across the room, she stood for a moment at the threshold of the sleeping house, her eyes tracing the familiar contours of the life she had built, piece by painstaking piece.

There was a quiet strength in the stillness, a silent witness to the fortitude that pulsed within her veins. The trials that had once seemed insurmountable now formed the bedrock of her resilience. Lisa breathed deeply, finding solace in the steady rhythm of her own heartbeat.

"Tomorrow is another day with fresh new beginnings," she whispered into the darkness, a vow forming with each breath. Her love for Ethan, Abigail, and little Julia was an unbreakable chain. She would not let this new tempest—the whispers, the past reemerging with Ava's return—shatter their world.

Turning away from the door, Lisa tiptoed back to her desk, running her fingers over the woodwork. It was more than just furniture; it was Oliver's craftsmanship, his passion carved into every groove and grain. The same hands that crafted such beauty held hers through every hardship.

"Oliver," she said softly to herself, "we'll weather this too."

She glanced out the window once more, where the stars twinkled like distant lighthouses guiding weary travelers home. They beckoned her to believe in the dawn of a new day, one that promised the chance for clarity and conversations steeped in understanding rather than anger.

With that tender hope cradling her heart, Lisa allowed the fatigue of the day to guide her body toward rest. She slipped beneath the covers of their bed without waking Oliver, feeling the linen cool against her skin.

As sleep finally claimed her, the edges of her thoughts softened, blurring into dreams. Dreams where the challenges they faced were but shadows, dissolving in the light of a steadfast resolve. Dreams of tomorrow, where the intricate dance of their lives continued, each step a testament to their shared journey and their shared love.

Chapter Six

Lisa's hands trembled slightly as she placed the "Closed" sign on the door of the cozy yet usually bustling cafe. The last customer had left, leaving behind a silence that seemed to amplify the cacophony of her thoughts. With her back pressed against the cool glass of the door, she closed her eyes and inhaled deeply, trying to steady the rapid beating of her heart.

The day's challenges weighed heavily upon her—unpaid bills, an unexpected shortage of coffee beans, a broken espresso machine—all piling atop the personal struggles that gnawed at her peace of mind. Her hair, usually neatly pinned up while working, cascaded in disheveled locks around her face as if mirroring the chaos within.

In this quiet moment, she allowed herself to feel it all—the fear, the exhaustion, the relentless pressure of being everything to everyone. A single tear escaped the corner of her eye, tracing a warm path down her cheek, but she quickly wiped it away with a determination born from years of overcoming adversities that would have shattered someone less resilient.

Outside, the quaint streets of the small town were bathed in the soft glow of the afternoon sun, casting long shadows that danced with the gentle breeze. Lyle Cooper, returning from his daily walk, noticed the subtle shift in Lisa's posture through the cafe window. His brow furrowed with concern for his neighbor, whom he had come to admire for her tenacity and warmth.

He approached the entrance, his footsteps soundless against the cobblestone path. Lyle paused for a fraction of a second, debating the intrusion, but his kind nature overruled any hesitation. He tapped lightly on the door, his grey-blue eyes filled with empathy, before walking in.

"Lisa?" Lyle's voice was a soothing balm, his presence an anchor in the storm threatening to sweep her away. "Are you okay?"

She opened her eyes, the sight of him offering a flicker of solace. Even in distress, she couldn't help but notice the genuine worry etched in the lines of his face —a face that had offered her countless smiles and words of wisdom.

"Hey, Lyle," she managed, her voice steadier than she felt. "I'm fine. I just needed a minute."

"Everyone needs a minute sometimes," Lyle said, his tone light yet laden with meaning. "Mind if I join you for yours?"

As he waited for her response, there was an electric charge in the air—and they both felt it.

"No, not at all. Do you want a cup of coffee?"

Lisa exhaled a shaky breath, her fingers absently tracing the rim of her coffee mug. Lyle pulled up a chair, his presence a quiet force in the whirlwind of Lisa's world. She looked into his eyes, finding an unexpected harbor there.

"I don't even know where to start," she confessed, the words tumbling out like the first drops before a storm. "The cafe, the woodwork shop, my kids… I can handle those, barely. But Ava—her being here—it's like juggling knives. And I'm just waiting to drop one."

"Life has a way of throwing more at us than we think we can handle," Lyle said, leaning forward, elbows resting on the table. His voice was steady, a counterpoint to the tremble in hers. "But you're not just anyone, Lisa. You're the woman who rebuilt her life from scratch, who protects her family like a lioness. You've got grit and heart, and you've turned this place," he gestured to the cozy cafe, "into a second home for half the town."

Lisa's eyes glistened, holding back a sea of emotions. Here was Lyle, who'd seen her at her best and worst, still believing in her when her own faith wavered. It was heartwarming and thrilling to be seen so clearly, and it ignited a flicker of hope within her chest.

"Maybe so," she whispered, allowing herself a small, grateful smile. "But sometimes, even lionesses need a moment to roar before they can fight again."

"Then roar, Lisa," Lyle encouraged with a gentle nudge, his gaze unwavering. "Roar until the skies clear and you remember the strength that's carried you this far. Because I have no doubt it'll carry you through whatever comes next."

His words were the very essence of encouragement, spoken with a conviction that seemed to pierce through the fog of her anxiety. At that moment, Lisa felt the raw edges of her resolve begin to knit back together, bolstered by the support of a friend who saw her not just as a neighbor in distress but as a warrior capable of weathering any attack from the outside world.

The next day, Lisa stood behind the counter, her hands gripping the edge as if it might anchor her amidst the chaos of her life. Oliver had left once again to spend time with his son—and Ava. He almost seemed relieved that he was able to get away when he told Lisa that same morning that he had promised to take them both fishing.

Both of them.

The bell above the door jingled gently—a reminder of the world moving on outside her swirling thoughts. She felt Lyle's presence before she saw him, a comforting solidity in the small space.

"Lisa," he began, his voice pulling her gaze upward. "I've been thinking." He paused, the lines around his eyes softening with concern. "You're carrying the weight of the world on your shoulders, and you do it with such grace. But even the strongest of us need a break."

She watched him and saw the sincerity etched into his weathered features. There was a tenderness there, a quiet longing that made her heart skip just slightly—not from romance, but from the sheer kindness he exuded.

"Julia's no trouble at all, and I'd be glad to watch her for a while. I can take her for a walk or even just sit with her while she plays. Take some time for yourself. You deserve that much, at least."

Her chest tightened. The offer was tempting—more than tempting, necessary. She needed space to breathe, to gather the scattered pieces of herself. And yet, her eyes flickered with hesitation, noting the way Lyle's gaze lingered on her, warm and perhaps wanting more than she could give.

"Are you sure? I don't want to impose—"

"Lisa," Lyle cut in, his voice firm yet gentle. "It's not imposing. It's me… offering a hand to a friend in need. Sometimes, we have to accept help to find our strength again."

The silent battle within her ebbed away, replaced by a wave of gratitude. Lyle's offer was a lifeline, one she was foolish even to consider refusing. Her shoulders relaxed, the tension that had coiled there dissipating like morning mist.

"Thank you, Lyle," she said, her voice barely louder than the refrigerator's hum behind her. "I... I would really appreciate that."

"Then, it's settled." He smiled, and she couldn't help but return it, however fleetingly. "Go on now. I'll close up here and take Julia for a stroll. You know she loves looking at the ducks down at Miller's Pond."

"Okay." She untied her apron, feeling the fabric slide through her fingers like sand. A momentary pause, and then she moved, stepping out from behind the counter with a resolve she hadn't felt in days.

"See you in a couple of hours," she called over her shoulder, pushing open the cafe door and letting the sunlight wash over her. The fresh air filled her lungs, a sweet promise of reprieve. As she walked the familiar path toward the ocean, what used to be her favorite place to go, Lisa allowed herself to envision an afternoon unfettered by demands or worries—an afternoon where the only company she kept was her own, heartwarming and thrilling in its simplicity.

Oliver's heart raced with a mix of excitement and nerves as he watched Daniel, his small frame dwarfed by the oversized fishing rod gripped in his tiny hands. The boy's focus was laser-sharp on the surface where the hook had disappeared, his tongue poking out slightly in concentration—a mirror image of Oliver's childhood habit. The peacefulness of the lakefront weaved seamlessly into their silent companionship, with only the occasional chirp of a nearby bird or the gentle lapping of water against the shore filling the quiet.

"No fishies?" Daniel finally asked, his voice hopeful but tinged with the innocence of doubt.

"Out here? There are tons of them," Oliver assured with a confident smile, though he knew that the real catch of the day would be the bond forming between them, not the fish at the end of the line.

The line plunged suddenly beneath the surface, and Daniel's eyes widened with surprise.

"I got one!" he yelled, excitement crackling through his words like static.

"Reel it in, buddy! Steady now," Oliver guided, standing close enough to assist but allowing Daniel the thrill of the moment. His hands hovered, ready to help, but the boy's determination surged through his tiny body, drawing the fish closer with every turn of the reel. Oliver stood behind him and helped pull it the last part, and Ava came up next to him, admiration in her eyes, while Oliver thought:

This is my family, too. We love each other.

The suspense hung in the air, thick as the humid summer breeze, until finally, with a triumphant grunt and help from both parents, Daniel pulled a small bass from the water. Its scales glinted like fresh coins in the sunlight, and Oliver couldn't suppress the pride swelling in his chest.

"Look at what you've caught!" Oliver exclaimed, ruffling Daniel's hair affectionately. "You're a natural, just like—"

He stopped short, the word "me" lingering unsaid on his lips. He was about to claim a connection he hadn't earned yet, but their shared grin, as wide and bright as the open sky, told him they were getting there.

"Just like his dad," Ava said.

"I guess, huh?" Oliver said.

She sent him a warm smile, and the twinkle in her eyes pulled him back to a life he had lived long ago—one filled with love and dreams for the future. A simpler life with no bills piling up and no sleepless nights of worry about money or the future.

With the afternoon waning, they left the comfort of the wharf's edge, trading the serene waters for the lively embrace of the nearby woods. They traipsed through the underbrush, playing an impromptu game of catch with pine cones that spiraled through the air, leaving laughter echoing among the trees.

"Bet you can't find me!" Daniel challenged, darting behind a thick oak with peals of laughter.

"Is that so?" Oliver called out playfully, pretending to search in the wrong direction, building suspense with each step. "Where could that little rascal be?"

"I don't know where he could be?" Ava said, playing along. "I guess he disappeared, huh?"

Peering around the tree, Oliver feigned surprise as he spotted the giggling boy. "Found you!" he announced, and Daniel leaped from his hiding spot, racing ahead with Oliver in pursuit.

Their exploration took them deeper into the forest, where shadows played tricks on the eye, and the thrill of the unknown nudged at Oliver's instincts. Every snapped twig underfoot or rustle in the foliage held the promise of adventure—or the whisper of danger. Oliver kept a watchful eye, the protective urge fierce and primal, even as he allowed Daniel the freedom to marvel at the wonders around them.

"Look, a deer!" Daniel whispered, tugging on Oliver's sleeve. He pointed toward a doe, observing them from a safe distance. "Look, Mommy!"

Their gazes locked with the creature's before she bounded away, her grace a fleeting ghost through the trees.

"Wow, did you see how fast she was?" Ava breathed in awe, her eyes alive with the spark Oliver remembered from their youth.

"Sure did," Oliver replied, his voice soft with the reverence of the moment. How many nights had he dreamed of being this close to her again? How many times had he been on his knees and prayed to God that he would get to look into those beautiful eyes again?

As the sun began its descent, painting the sky in hues of gold and crimson, they made their way back to the edge of the woods, the bond between them as tangible as the earth beneath their feet. Oliver looked down at Daniel, his hand securely wrapped around the boy's, and felt an unspoken promise settle in his soul.

"Best day ever," Daniel declared, his smile holding the world.

"Absolutely," Oliver agreed, his heart full, knowing

that days like these were the foundation of something profound—an unexpected family growing stronger with every shared heartbeat.

The wooden toy boat skimmed across the pond's surface, its sails catching the last rays of sunlight as it ventured bravely into the unknown. Oliver crouched beside Daniel, both sets of eyes tracking the vessel with a mix of pride and anticipation.

"Think it'll make it to the other side?" Ava's voice was laced with excitement.

"Absolutely," Oliver replied, confidence buoying his words. "You made a fine ship, Captain Daniel."

Daniel beamed up at him, and in that instant, Oliver felt a surge of warmth that went beyond the afternoon sun. He saw not just the boy before him but the young man he might one day become—the laughter lines already etching the corners of his eyes a testament to the joy he brought. This connection, this moment, was more than Oliver had ever hoped for when he imagined having a son.

"Can I tell you a secret?" Daniel suddenly asked.

"Of course," Oliver said, leaning in closer.

"I'm glad to be here," Daniel whispered, a shy smile dancing on his lips. I like having you as my dad. I like my family." He said it while grabbing his mother's hand in his other hand and pulling them all close. Oliver lifted his gaze, and his eyes met Ava's. He felt his heart beat faster as he stared at her lips, wondering what it would feel like to kiss them again.

You can't. Think of Lisa. Think of the children.

Oliver's throat tightened with emotion, the title of "dad" echoing in his heart like a sacred vow. This was no longer about filling an absent role; it was about building something new, something precious.

"Me too, buddy," he managed to say, his voice barely above a whisper. "Me too."

As they watched the boat reach the safety of the far shore, Oliver knew they had crossed their uncharted waters, navigating toward a future filled with hope and the promise of family.

Lisa turned the corner onto Main Street, the familiar sights of her small town wrapping around her like a well-worn quilt. She drew a deep breath, the air infused with the scent of pine and the faintest hint of Lyle's aftershave—a reminder of his comforting presence. He had listened without judgment, offered help without hesitation, and, in doing so, had given her the most precious gift: time for herself.

Her mind felt clearer, her spirit lighter, as she approached the pond behind the bakery. And that's when she saw them. Together. All three of them—holding hands. She felt her heart skip a beat and a shriek get caught in her throat. It felt like someone had punched her in the gut.

There they all were, as a family, enjoying each

other, and she couldn't even be angry about it. The boy deserved a family, too. He deserved a father just as much as everyone else.

I'm losing him. I can feel it. It hurts.

She backed up and walked away, letting them enjoy the moment, her heart shattered. She hurried home, where her children had come back from school. Their smiles and laughter were what she needed right now.

"Mom!" Ethan and Abigail chorused, rushing to envelop her in a tangle of limbs and excited chatter.

"Hey, there," she smiled, hugging them tight, the weight in her chest easing further with each passing second. "Did you have fun with Lyle?"

"Yep, we played games, and he even helped me with my homework," Abigail beamed, and Ethan nodded enthusiastically.

"Good," Lisa said, gratitude lacing her words. "He's a good man."

She walked Lyle out to the door. "Thank you for this. It was truly a needed gift."

"You're welcome," he said with a smile. "Anytime. I'm right next door if you need me again. I won't mind taking care of the little one now and then. She's fun and reminds me of my niece when she was that age. I never had children myself, but I always babysat her for my sister."

"I might take you up on that," Lisa said.

He pulled her into a hug, and as their bodies touched, Lisa felt a spark rush through her. When they pulled apart, Lyle looked into her eyes, his gaze as warm as the embrace. "You're a remarkable woman," he said. "You deserve the best."

"Thank you," she said, blushing.

She watched as Lyle left and waved from the window, her heart confused and fluttering. What was happening to her? To them?

It didn't take long before Oliver came home, too. He was alone, and it pleased her to see him, even though it hurt deeply inside.

"Everything okay?" Oliver asked, his gaze meeting hers, searching for any sign of distress.

"Yes," she forced a smile. "It's better than okay," she assured him, keeping her voice steady. "Thanks to Lyle, I got the break I didn't know I needed. He took Julia for a while and helped the older kids with their homework. And it looks like you had a pretty good time as well."

"Best time," Oliver corrected with a wink, and she could see the joy and fulfillment in his eyes. It hurt more than anything.

"Then let's keep the good times rolling," Lisa suggested, trying to keep the mood up and not let him know she was devastated.

"Who's up for a game night?" she announced, earning cheers from the children.

"Game on," Oliver agreed, his smile matching hers as they gathered around the table.

Lisa paused at the living room threshold, her eyes taking in the tableau before her. It was late afternoon, and she had just closed the café for the day. Oliver and Daniel were sprawled on the floor, surrounded by wooden blocks and half-constructed towers, their laughter echoing off the walls like a sweet melody. To her joy, Ava wasn't there. It was just the two of them. It was a heartwarming scene that tugged at the strings of her heart with an intensity she hadn't expected. She leaned against the doorframe, a contented sigh escaping her lips as she watched them play.

"Watch this, Lisa!" Daniel's voice chimed, full of excitement. The boy was clutching a block, his small brow furrowed in concentration. With a swift movement, he placed it atop the teetering tower, his tongue peeking out from the corner of his mouth. The structure wobbled precariously but held firm. "I did it!"

"Nice work, champ," Oliver praised, his eyes sparkling with pride. He ruffled Daniel's hair, a gesture so fatherly it sent a shiver through Lisa.

"Did I miss all the fun?" Lisa asked, her voice warm yet carrying a hint of playful accusation.

"Never," Oliver replied, getting to his feet and brushing off his pants. "We saved the best for last."

"Moments like these," Lisa began, stepping into the room, her gaze flitting between Oliver and Daniel, "they're what life's all about, aren't they?"

"Absolutely," Oliver said, his smile broadening as he extended his hand to her.

Lisa took it, allowing him to pull her onto the floor beside them. Her heart swelled as she nestled into their circle, the simple joy of the moment wrapping around her like a cozy blanket. It was thrilling how seamlessly they fit together, creating a picture of domestic bliss that seemed almost too good to be true.

"Building memories, one block at a time," she quipped, reaching for a wooden piece to add to the burgeoning metropolis they were constructing.

"Exactly."

Oliver's voice held a note of something deeper and more profound as if every shared laugh and toppled tower cemented the bond he was building with Daniel.

As they continued their architectural endeavors, Lisa couldn't help but marvel at the ease with which Oliver had stepped into this unexpected role. There was an undercurrent of suspense, a silent question hanging in the air—where would this connection lead? Would he want to go back to Ava? To rekindle what had been lost? To become the family he had wanted so desperately and that the boy needed?

For now, she pushed those thoughts aside, focusing on the present, the joyous sounds filling her home, and the love that seemed to grow with every passing second.

"Look at us," she whispered, more to herself than the others. "We're really doing this, aren't we?"

Oliver caught her eye, his gaze shimmering with unspoken emotion. "Yeah, we are," he confirmed, squeezing her hand gently. "And it's just the beginning."

The golden hues of the setting sun filtered through the curtains, casting a warm glow on the makeshift fort under the dining table. Giggles and hushed whispers escaped the blanket-draped sanctuary as Lisa playfully searched for the hidden occupants, her heart swelling with affection for this impromptu game of hide-and-seek that had captivated them all afternoon.

"Gotcha!" she exclaimed as she peeked beneath the drapes. She found Oliver and Daniel entwined in an embrace of laughter, the boy's face alight with delight. The simple act of joyous discovery felt like a treasure, and each shared smile between them was a gem to be cherished.

Their play was interrupted by the front door swinging open, the familiar sound of school bags hitting the floor announcing Ethan and Abigail's return. The children burst into the room, and their youthful curiosity was immediately piqued by the presence of the little stranger amidst their family tableau.

"Mom, why is he here?" Ethan asked, his green eyes wide with intrigue as he took in the sight of Daniel still nestled close to Oliver.

"Because he is Oliver's son," Lisa said warmly, watching her children's reactions closely. Abigail, ever the embodiment of her mother's warmth, approached Daniel with a welcoming grin while Ethan hung back slightly, protective instincts flaring gently.

The arrival of another visitor soon overshadowed their inquiries. The door opened again to reveal Lyle, cradling baby Julia in his arms, her tiny fingers wrapped around his finger—a silent testament to the trust they placed in him. His gentle smile offered solace, and his arrival seemed to fill the space with a comforting familiarity.

"I'm sad to have to let go of this little one. We had fun today, but I think she's hungry," Lyle said, his gaze lingering on Lisa just a moment too long before he handed over the cooing bundle.

"Would you stay for dinner?" Lisa asked, her voice laden with gratitude. His assistance was a balm to the frenetic energy that now enveloped the house.

"Wouldn't miss it," Lyle replied, the corners of his eyes crinkling with genuine pleasure.

"Ava will be here soon, too," Oliver said. "To pick up Daniel. Maybe she can stay for dinner as well? Like one big happy family?"

Lisa cleared her throat, waited for a beat to answer, and made sure her voice was steady. Once it was, she said:

"Of course. That would be delightful."

As they gathered around the kitchen table, the scent of pot roast mingled with the hearty aroma of baked potatoes filled the air. Plates clinked, and glasses chimed in a symphony of domesticity. But beneath the mundane, a thread of tension wove itself into the fabric of the evening.

Lyle, seated too close to Lisa for Oliver's comfort, cast knowing looks and gentle jibes that danced dangerously close to revealing his unspoken desires.

"Quite the catch, isn't she?" he teased Oliver, nodding toward Ava, whose presence was filled with unspoken words and lingering glances from Oliver.

Oliver's laugh felt forced, his hand instinctively reaching for Lisa's, seeking reassurance. The moment held a spark of suspense as if Lyle's words were the flint threatening to ignite a fire of jealousy and doubt.

Lisa felt the air thicken, her pulse quickening with the awareness of Lyle's intentions and the precarious balance they now navigated. Yet amid the discomfort, her resolve hardened. She would not let this meal—this day of newfound connections—be marred by the complexities of adult emotions.

"Let's toast," Lisa suggested, raising her glass to cut through the growing unease. "To family, old and new, and to the memories we're creating together."

Glasses clinked in agreement, a clear chime in the silence that had begun to settle. For a fleeting moment, as they drank to her words, the tension dissipated, and the promise of heartwarming unity shone brighter than any challenge ahead. But the moment was only fleeting.

The clatter of dishes being cleared echoed in the dining room as twilight cast its subtle glow through the windows. Ava's silhouette appeared at the kitchen door, a soft halo of evening light framing her figure, and Lisa felt an inexplicable tightness grip her chest. She watched from across the room as Oliver stepped forward, his movements careful and deliberate, to hand Daniel his jacket.

"Thanks for letting me stay for dinner," Ava chirped. "That was really nice of you. You didn't have to do that."

"Of course," Lisa said, her voice strained. "We're family now."

"See you soon, buddy," Oliver said, ruffling the boy's messy hair, a fatherly gesture that pulled at Lisa's heart.

Ava's smile was a mix of gratitude and something deeper, leaving an uncomfortable prickle under Lisa's skin. She caught Oliver's gaze lingering a moment too long on Ava's face as he walked her out, and although he turned away, the image seared into Lisa's mind, stoking embers of jealousy she wished didn't exist.

Lyle, ever observant, edged closer to Lisa, his presence a steady warmth at her side. "You see that, don't you?" he murmured, his voice a low rumble. "The way he looks at her… It's like you're not even in the room."

Lisa's throat tightened, the words hitting too close to home. She wanted to dismiss them, to believe in the trust she and Oliver had built, but doubt crept in like wisps of fog on a clear night.

"Maybe I'm imagining things," she whispered back, more to convince herself than to confide in Lyle.

"Or maybe you're seeing things clearly for the first time," Lyle said, his tone gentle yet laced with an edge that suggested he knew far more than he let on.

As Ava ushered Daniel out the door with a soft promise to return soon, Lyle reached for Lisa's hand, guiding her toward the back entrance. They walked in silence, the tension between them palpable, a current of unspoken thoughts and feelings charging the air.

At the doorway, under the porch light casting shadows around them, Lyle turned to face her. His eyes held a depth of emotion that made her breath hitch. Before she could react, he leaned in, pressing a kiss to her lips, lingering just a heartbeat longer than necessary.

"Thank you for dinner," he said, his voice barely above a whisper.

Lisa pulled back slightly, meeting his gaze. "Lyle, I'm with Oliver," she stated firmly, despite the fluttering in her stomach and the uncertainty clouding her heart. Lyle was a very handsome man, and she was attracted to him, but she loved Oliver.

"For now," Lyle replied, his smile hinting at both resignation and challenge. He stepped back, nodding once before turning to walk down the path, leaving Lisa standing in the doorway. Her emotions were a tangled knot of gratitude, confusion, and an undeniable thrill of what-ifs.

She closed the door slowly, leaning against it, the cool wood grounding her as she took a deep, steadying breath. The evening had ended on a note she hadn't anticipated, leaving her with a sense of fear for what lay ahead; somehow, it felt both thrilling and terrifying in its potential.

Chapter Seven

Lisa sat at the kitchen table with a steaming mug of coffee cradled in her hands. The gentle hum of the refrigerator accompanied her thoughts as she gazed out the window at the sleepy town coming to life in the soft morning light. She couldn't shake the tension that had settled between her and Oliver like an unwelcome guest. Their connection, once as seamless as the horizon where the sky met the sea, had been frayed by countless worries and silent meals.

The wavy brown strands of her hair fell across her face as she leaned forward, her resolve hardening. It was time to weave those frayed ends back together—a special evening, she thought, one carefully crafted with threads of romance and nostalgia—perhaps it could remind Oliver of the love that had once felt as vast and deep as the ocean he so missed.

With a determined sip of her coffee, Lisa opened her laptop and began her quest. Her fingers danced over the keys, eyes flickering across the screen as she delved into the art of unforgettable date nights. She envisioned Oliver's smile, the one that reached his ocean-blue eyes and warmed her faster than the midday sun. Remembering how he would speak reverently of his days on the fishing boat, the salty breeze tangling his dark hair, she typed in "ocean-themed evenings" and hit enter.

A plethora of ideas flooded the screen, and Lisa's pulse quickened. Each click was a step closer to the perfect night—a harmonious blend of thrill and romance that would reignite their spark. She imagined transforming their backyard into a seaside sanctuary, complete with the sounds of lapping waves and the scent of the sea. Or perhaps they could have a cozy indoor picnic, a starfish-patterned blanket spread across the living room floor, surrounded by candlelit jars filled with sand and seashells.

Her heart swelled at the thought of Oliver's woodworking tools shaping something beautiful from raw wood, so she added a personal touch to her mental blueprint: a hand-carved memento for him to find, a symbol of their enduring partnership despite the storms they weathered.

As Lisa's plans took shape, her excitement surged like the tide. It wasn't just about the evening; it was a sign of hope, a declaration that no matter how rough the waters, they could navigate them together. She jotted down notes meticulously, considering every detail—from the playlist echoing the calls of seabirds to the menu reminiscent of their first seaside date.

The thrill of anticipation mingled with suspense.

Would her efforts be enough to bridge the distance that had crept between them? Could a single evening wash away the strain of financial burdens and past insecurities? Only time would tell, but Lisa was not one to shy away from a challenge. With a love as deep as theirs, she was willing to dive into unknown depths.

Lisa's fingers fluttered through her closet, and there was a sense of urgency in her movements. She pulled out a navy blue dress that Oliver loved. Its fabric flowed like waves when she walked, and she knew it would bring a smile to his face. She carefully laid it across the bed, smoothing any wrinkles with tender strokes.

The house was quiet with the kids at a sleepover, even Julia, who was at Maggie's for the night, leaving room for romance to blossom without interruption. In the kitchen, Lisa set about crafting the ambiance. She scattered sand across the countertop, interspersed with small shells they had collected together on better days. The flicker of candlelight bounced off a hand-carved wooden whale, one Oliver had made long ago but never left the studio—a testament to their shared journey and Oliver's love for woodworking.

Her heart beat in rhythm with the melodies of seabirds emanating softly from the speakers, carefully chosen to evoke memories of their early days by the water's edge. Every detail was a thread, weaving together past and present as Lisa filled the room with scents of salt and pine, a harmony of their lives entwined.

With dinner simmering—seafood chowder, Oliver's favorite—Lisa stepped into her dress, the fabric hugging her figure. A glance in the mirror confirmed her readiness, but it was the flush of anticipation on her cheeks that truly completed the look.

She was lighting the last candle when she heard the key turn in the front door. Her pulse quickened. This was the moment of truth.

"Lisa?" Oliver called out with a hint of curiosity as he stepped inside.

He had been at the inn with Ava and Daniel all day again, and now it was Lisa's turn to have him to herself.

"Surprise," Lisa said, her voice barely above a whisper, yet it carried clearly through the transformed space.

Oliver stood in the doorway, his tall frame silhouetted against the fading light outside. His eyes swept over the scene before him, widening in recognition of each lovingly placed detail—the scent of the ocean, the wooden whale, the soft music—and finally settling on Lisa herself.

"Wow," he breathed out, taking it all in. "This is… incredible."

His words were simple, but the emotion behind them ran deep. He moved closer, reaching out to trace a finger along the grain of the wooden whale that Lisa had sanded down and perfected, a silent acknowledgment of the effort Lisa had poured into this evening.

"Thank you," he murmured, wrapping his arms around her. "I can't remember the last time we did something like this."

"Neither can I," Lisa admitted, the warmth of his embrace melting away the last vestiges of doubt, at least for a little while.

There was a thrill in the air, a current of suspense that danced between them as they stood there, holding each other at the precipice of the night ahead. It was heartwarming and exciting, thrilling and suspenseful —all at once.

Lisa led Oliver by the hand to their moonlit sanctuary on the beach, her heart pounding in sync with the gentle lap of waves against the shore. The blanket she had spread out was soft beneath their feet, a patch-work quilt of memories pieced together with love and care. Above them, a billion stars twinkled like diamond dust scattered across an obsidian canvas, the constellations telling tales as old as time.

"Look at this," Oliver whispered, his voice hushed in reverence to the natural cathedral they stood within. His gaze lingered on the picnic basket, the candles flickering in glass jars, and the simple yet elegant spread of homemade delicacies Lisa had prepared.

She watched, basking in the glow of his apprecia-tion, as he bent down to examine the spread—a selec-tion of his favorite cheeses, the olives he'd mentioned once in passing, and fresh bread still warm from the oven. She'd even managed to find that wine he'd raved about after trying it on some trip to a vineyard many years ago—a minor miracle in the tiny coastal town they called home.

"Lisa, you did all this for us?" he asked, turning to her with those deep-set eyes that never failed to see right through her.

"Of course," Lisa replied, her voice steady though her nerves fluttered like the wings of a caged bird. "I wanted tonight to be special, a night where it's just you, me, and the sea."

They settled onto the quilt, the sand molding to their forms as if embracing old friends. With each sip of wine and each shared smile, the space between them filled with an intoxicating blend of warmth and longing. They ate slowly, savoring not just the food but the rarity of the moment—undistracted, unhurried, unburdened.

Oliver reached out, brushing a stray lock of hair behind Lisa's ear. His fingertips grazed her skin with a tender touch, sending shivers down her spine. Their eyes met, and the world fell away momentarily, leaving only the two of them suspended in time.

"Thank you for this," he said softly, his words carrying the weight of gratitude and something deeper that spoke to the core of his being—a man who yearned for the simplicity of life on the water, now anchored by love and responsibility.

"Every detail, Lisa… it's perfect."

"Only the best for you," she responded, leaning

into his embrace. The connection between them sparked and sizzled, igniting a flame that seemed to dance with the candlelight, casting shadows that played upon their faces, hinting at the passion smoldering just beneath the surface.

Their laughter mingled with the symphony of the ocean's lullaby, and as they sat there, under the watchful gaze of the heavens, Lisa and Oliver found themselves navigating the tides of their own hearts—thrilled by the journey, warmed by their closeness, and held in suspense by the promise of what the night might bring.

The waves softly caressed the shore, their rhythmic hush a gentle accompaniment to the clink of cutlery and murmur of conversation. Lisa, her face aglow in the flickering candlelight, reached across the picnic blanket to refill Oliver's glass with wine, her hand trembling ever so slightly.

"Oliver," she began, her voice barely louder than the sea breeze, "I've been thinking about us, about everything we've been through recently." Her eyes searched his, reflecting the stars in the night sky.

He caught her hand, holding it firmly yet gently. "I know, love. It's been… challenging, to say the least."

The furrows in his brow deepened as he paused, turning his gaze toward the dark expanse of the ocean that once was his home and workplace. "Sometimes, I wonder if starting the business was the right move.

The financial strain is—" He stopped, his voice trailing off into the sound of the waves.

"More than we expected," Lisa finished for him. She gave his hand a reassuring squeeze. "But we have each other, and we'll get through this. We always do."

Oliver nodded, but his eyes held so much worry. "And then there's Ava and Daniel. Their arrival in town—it's stirred up a lot of emotions I hadn't antici-pated." The words hung between them, heavy like the air before a thunderstorm.

"Her being your past complicates things," Lisa admitted, her chest tight with an unspoken fear. "And Daniel… he's such a sweet boy." She trailed off, leaving Oliver to fill the silence.

"It's not just that Ava was my first love; it's that she needed a father figure for the boy, and I couldn't turn her away, not with Daniel looking up at me with those big eyes, so like—" He swallowed, unable to finish the thought.

"Like yours," Lisa finished softly, understanding the unvoiced connection. "It doesn't change how I feel about you, Ollie. But sometimes, I worry it changes how you feel about us."

"Lisa, no," he said quickly, his expression earnest. "You and your kids, and Julia, you're my present and future. It's just… the added pressure makes me feel like I'm failing you somehow."

"Never," she whispered fiercely. Lisa leaned forward, her resolve shining in her eyes. "I still believe in us. Don't you?"

"Of course I do," he replied, but his hesitance

betrayed the war within him—a battle between devotion and doubt.

The ocean continued its timeless lullaby, indifferent to the human hearts that beat in sync with its tides—two souls entwined by love yet buffeted by the relentless winds of circumstance.

The beach was secluded, a hidden gem away from prying eyes and the bustle of their small-town life. Lisa watched Oliver, the corners of her mouth lifting in a soft smile that crinkled the corners of her warm eyes. They had come here for an escape, a brief interlude where the soothing symphony of waves could wash away the complexities of their shared past. It seemed to have worked. She felt more at ease than she had in a long time.

"This is perfect," she said, her voice mingling with the rhythmic crashing of the surf as she tucked her legs beneath her. Her shoulder-length brown hair fluttered slightly in the sea breeze, strands occasionally dancing across her face.

Oliver sat beside her, his well-built frame sinking comfortably into the sand. His eyes reflected the expanse of the ocean before them—a mirror to the depth of the life they had built together. He let out a contented sigh, the tension in his shoulders dissipating in the salt-tinged air.

"Remember the first time we came here?" Lisa

began, leaning into Oliver's solid presence. "It feels like lifetimes ago, yet here we are."

"Every day with you is a new chapter, Lisa."

Oliver's voice was soft but carried the weight of his conviction. "We've weathered more storms than I can count, but somehow, it made the calm even more… precious."

Lisa nodded, her fingers absentmindedly tracing patterns on the blanket, each line a silent testament to their resilience. "We've built something incredible, Ollie. A family, a business…." She paused, her gaze flicking up to meet his. "A life."

"Built on trust," he added, his hand covering hers, halting her movements. "And love. We fought for this peace every step of the way."

"Especially when it felt like the world was against us." The memories of her violent past crept into the edges of her consciousness, but Lisa pushed them away, focusing instead on the man beside her, the embodiment of safety and devotion.

"Against us, maybe. But never strong enough to break us." Oliver's voice held a firm edge of protectiveness. "We've got each other, and that's more than enough to take on any storm."

Their conversation flowed effortlessly, a stream of shared memories and quiet acknowledgments of the struggles they had overcome. With each word, their bond seemed to strengthen, the undercurrent of gratitude for one another pulsing like the heartbeat of the earth itself.

"Thank you," Lisa whispered, at last, her words

barely louder than the hush of the surrounding nature. "For being my harbor in the chaos."

"Always," Oliver replied, his promise as steadfast as the horizon line. "I love you, Lisa."

"I love you too, Oliver. More than I ever thought possible."

&

In the waning light, Oliver's hand found Lisa's, his calloused fingers weaving through hers with practiced ease. The intimate gesture, so familiar and yet always thrilling, anchored her to the here and now, a bulwark against the specter of her past fears. Their hands fit together as if molded from the same clay, the lines of their lives eternally intertwined.

"Remember when we first held hands?" Oliver's low voice broke the silence, his thumb tracing the back of her hand in a slow, deliberate motion. His eyes were like dark pools that searched her face for memories shared and cherished.

Lisa felt her heartbeat quicken, not just from the recollection but from the intense gaze he held on her.

"It was the moment I knew."

"Knew what?" Lisa teased, though the depth of emotion in Oliver's expression sent ripples of anticipation through her.

"That you were going to change everything." The earnestness in his tone wrapped around her like a warm blanket.

The moonlight danced across Oliver's features,

highlighting the strength in his jawline—the jawline that had tensed in determination whenever life threw hurdles their way. It softened now with tenderness, a testament to the gentleness that belied his rugged exterior.

Before she knew it, Lisa found herself leaning in, the magnetic pull between them as undeniable as the tides that lapped at the shore. Her lips met his in a tender brush, a whisper of a kiss that seemed to still the world around them. It was a prelude, a promise of connection that spoke volumes in the fleeting touch.

Oliver's response was a surge of warmth, a spark that caught and kindled into a flame. The simple caress deepened, and Lisa reveled in the sensation, the desire that awakened with every gentle press of their mouths. In this kiss lay the echoes of every challenge they had faced, every victory they had celebrated, every quiet night they had clung to each other, seeking solace in the sanctuary of their love.

As their lips parted, the air between them felt charged with unspoken emotion. Lisa could feel the pulse of excitement threading through the serenity of the evening. The thrill of what lay ahead was palpable, a thrilling undercurrent to the steady beat of their joined hearts. They were a fortress of two against the mysteries of the night, their love a light that would guide them through whatever darkness might come.

The world around them seemed to dissolve as Oliver drew Lisa closer, their kiss deepening beyond the tender exploration of moments ago. This was a fervent clash of lips and tongues, a dance that spoke of hunger edged with the sweetest of promises. Each breath they shared stoked the fires within, and Lisa felt herself sinking into the intensity of their connection, her heart pounding in exhilarating harmony with the crashing waves.

Oliver's hands began a tentative journey across the landscape of Lisa's body, his touch lighting paths of fiery sensation that left no room for thought, only feeling. Her skin hummed beneath his fingertips as he traced the contours of her frame, each curve memorized and worshipped in the silent language of lovers. The sensation of his caresses sent shivers cascading down her spine, a tide of pleasure that crested with each tender stroke.

Lisa's awareness of the beach, of the softly fading light, all faded into insignificance as she surrendered to the thrill of Oliver's touch. The very sand they lay upon seemed to mold itself to their forms, cradling them in its warm embrace as if even the earth beneath conspired to draw them closer together.

Here with Oliver, every scar of her past was soothed, every shadow chased away by the strength of their shared devotion. And as the stars above danced in hues of passion, they found themselves lost in a world where only their love existed—a haven from the maelstrom of life, a fortress built not of wood or stone but of unbreakable bonds forged through trials and tenderness alike.

Lisa's fingers wove through Oliver's dark hair, gripping gently as she drew him nearer. The texture was familiar, a comforting contrast to the intensity of their embrace. With each passing moment, the world around them diminished until there was nothing but the heat of their bodies and the rhythm of their hearts beating in sync. They pressed against one another, two souls cast adrift on a sea of passion, finding a harbor in each other's arms.

Their kiss finally broke, breaths escaping in ragged synchrony, a testament to the fervor that had consumed them. Lisa's lips felt tender and swollen with desire, and her chest heaved as she tried to steady her breathing. She could feel the rapid pulse at Oliver's throat as he began to scatter kisses across her jawline, each one a small spark setting her skin alight. His lips whispered down her neck, leaving a trail of warmth that pooled deep within her.

As Oliver's mouth found the delicate slope of her collarbone, Lisa tilted her head back, her eyes fluttering closed in silent invitation. Each kiss was a promise, a silent oath of protection and love from a man whose strength and devotion had become the bedrock upon which her once-shattered trust was rebuilt. The sensation was dizzying, a thrilling cascade that teased the edges of suspense, for every touch held the potential of deeper intimacy, the unspoken mysteries of desires yet to be fulfilled.

The murmur of waves crashing against the shore

underscored the urgency between them, each ebb and flow mirroring the tumultuous emotions that surged through Lisa's veins. Here, nestled against the heart of the man who had pieced back together the fragments of her past, Lisa found not only the thrill of romance but an exhilarating sense of safety that made her soul sing. With his wood-worn hands and eyes that held oceans of sorrow turned to joy, Oliver was her anchor amidst life's storms.

In this stolen moment, Lisa marveled at the beauty of their union. Fear and doubt were distant memories, replaced by the suspenseful anticipation of a future painted in broad strokes of love and excitement. Oliver's presence was a reassuring weight against her, a thrilling reminder of the journey they had embarked upon together—a journey that promised as much heartwarming discovery as it did thrilling adventure.

The bright light from the moon wrapped around them like a lover's embrace as Oliver's lips continued their tender exploration of Lisa's skin. The soft undertones of salt and sand mingled with the warmth between them, creating an intoxicating ambiance that heightened every sensation. With each brush of Oliver's mouth against the tender nape of her neck, Lisa let out involuntary gasps, her body responding to his touch with quivers of excitement.

"Oliver," she breathed, her voice trembling not from cold but from the potent mix of desire and anticipation. Each kiss was a promise, each caress a vow, as if he were reaffirming their bond with the gentle urgency of his touch. His hands, those skilled conduits of both creation and tenderness, roamed over her with a reverence that belied his robust exterior.

There was a deliberate slowness to the way they undressed each other, a savoring of the moment that made it all the more intense. It was as though with each article of clothing that fell away, they were peeling back layers of their souls, exposing the raw, unguarded depths of their love. Oliver's fingers traced the contours of her form, pausing at the hollows and curves he knew as intimately as the grains of wood he so lovingly shaped.

Lisa matched his movements, her hands exploring the landscape of his body with equal parts wonder and familiarity. As fabric gave way to skin, they stood there, two beings stripped of pretense, bared before the elements and each other. Their naked forms glowed, the sea breeze kissing their skin, and for a fleeting second, the world outside their cocoon of passion ceased to exist.

The suspense of the moment stretched out, thrumming with the pulse of the waves, the air between them charged with heartwarming electricity. It was thrilling, the unveiling of themselves not just in body but in spirit, a testament to the trust and the unbreakable connection they had forged through trials and tenderness alike. This was their dance, a rhythm set to the timeless tune of the ocean, a harmony of hearts that promised to beat in unison through what-ever mysteries lay ahead.

§

Oliver's hands cradled Lisa's face as they descended together back onto the soft picnic blanket, a tapestry interwoven with the threads of their past and the promise of their future. The grains of sand beneath them were witnesses to this gentle collision of souls, each particle a silent keeper of their secrets and shared dreams.

With every touch, every caress, Oliver sought out the unspoken wishes that danced behind Lisa's eyes, eyes that held stories of resilience, eyes that had seen both the shadows and the light. In turn, Lisa mapped the landscape of Oliver's well-built form with her fingertips, and the strength in his arms that had hoisted fishing nets was now used to pull her closer into his embrace. Their movements were fluid, a choreography of desire that unfolded with each breath, each whisper of skin against skin.

The world around them fell away, leaving only the raw intimacy of their union, an exploration that was as much about giving as it was receiving. His lips found her pulse point, a tender area that quivered at his touch, eliciting a soft moan that floated away on the breeze. Lisa, in response, traced the line of Oliver's jaw, a subtle reminder of the rugged coastline that had shaped him and led him to her.

As their bodies moved in perfect harmony, they

discovered new peaks of pleasure, rising and falling with the tide. They were lost in the moment, two hearts entangled in a dance as old as time itself yet as fresh and exhilarating as the first light of dawn.

In this sacred space where the sea met the land, Oliver and Lisa surrendered to the depth of their emotions, riding the cresting waves to reach the zenith of their shared ecstasy. It was a vulnerable surrender, yet one fortified by the trust and devotion that had been the cornerstone of their bond. It was a testament to the unwavering love that tethered them together even as they soared.

Oliver's chest heaved, and Lisa nestled against him, her head on his shoulder, feeling the steady beat of his heart against her ear—a rhythmic affirmation of life and love. They lay together on the picnic blanket, a tangle of limbs and whispered sighs, both savoring the warmth that radiated between them.

"Lisa," Oliver murmured, his voice barely louder than the distant call of the sea birds, "I never knew… I could feel like this." His fingers traced lazy circles on her back, mapping the landscape of her skin as if committing each detail to memory.

Lisa lifted her head, her hazel eyes reflecting the depth of her emotions. The vulnerability she often guarded so fiercely seemed to melt away in Oliver's embrace.

"Me either," she confessed, the words spilling out like a secret long held close. "In your arms, I find strength and peace. I love you more than I ever thought possible."

He tightened his hold on her, a protective instinct mingling with the tenderness that filled his chest—an echo of the waves' relentless persistence.

Their gazes locked, a silent pact forming in the space between them. It was a promise of constancy amid the unpredictability of their small-town life—a vow to face any threat that dared to disrupt the tranquility they had fought so hard to build.

"Let's cherish every moment," Lisa said, her voice tinged with a blend of excitement and suspense that mirrored the thrill of their shared journey. "Every sunrise, every storm, every quiet day… everything with you is where I want to be."

Oliver traced the line of Lisa's collarbone with a gentle finger. The ocean hummed its eternal song, waves crashing rhythmically against the shore as if to honor their secluded union. Side by side on the picnic blanket, their limbs woven together in a tender lattice, they lay beneath an ever-deepening sky.

The tranquility of the moment was profound, yet it carried undercurrents of thrill—the kind that danced along one's spine when danger had passed but might lurk just beyond the horizon. In this quiet afterglow, the world outside their cocoon seemed both distant and charged with potential secrets.

Oliver felt the warmth of her skin against his own, a contrast to the cool breeze that began to sweep across the beach—a reminder of nature's dual capacity for comfort and threat. His arms tightened around her, not just in affection, but in an instinctual need to protect. The scent of the salty air mingled with the remnants of their lovemaking, creating an aroma unique to this moment, this shared chapter in their lives.

"It's getting cold," he said. "I'll make a fire."

The crackling of the firewood in the makeshift pit on the beach provided a stark contrast to the chilling silence that soon fell between them. The lovemaking was over, and now they were both lost in their thoughts. The once comforting glow now cast elongated shadows, mirroring the growing rift between them, the uncertainty she felt when looking at him, the insecurity she couldn't escape. Ava was so beautiful. They had a shared history. They had a child. Could she really trust his promises? She had seen them together. Holding hands. Looking like a family. Lisa watched as Oliver poked at the embers with a stick, his movements brusque, his jaw set tight.

"Ollie, we can't keep pretending," Lisa's voice broke through the quiet, her words trembling like the orange flames before them. "This… us trying to juggle it all—it's tearing at the seams."

Oliver's hand stilled, and he turned to face her, his turmoil evident in the crease between his brows. A shift had occurred in his usually so gentle eyes.

"What do you want me to say, Lisa? That I miss the open ocean so much it gnaws at me every time I pass the harbor? Or that every night I lie awake fearing I'll never be enough for this family?"

"Is that truly what you think?" Her heart skipped a beat, the raw honesty in his voice piercing through her defenses. "That you're not enough?"

"Isn't it obvious?" He stood up abruptly, his silhouette a dark figure against the backdrop of the silver-lit sea. "Every day is a reminder of what I've given up— and what I still can't provide."

"Your sacrifices haven't gone unnoticed, Ollie." Lisa rose to meet him, her eyes glistening with unshed tears. "But I fear I'm losing you, not to the sea, but to your ghosts, to your past."

"Here we go again. You mean Ava, right? And Daniel. I know it's gotten complicated, but I don't know how else to deal with it. But it will never be enough, will it? For any of you? Maybe it was easier when it was just me and the waves," he admitted, the confession cutting into her like a shard of driftwood. "I didn't have to worry about failing anyone else."

"Love isn't about tallying successes or failures!" Lisa's voice rose, passion fueling her words. "It's about facing these storms together, not letting them erode what we've built."

"Built?" Oliver laughed bitterly. "We're barely holding on. Every new bill and unexpected expense feels like another wave ready to pull us under."

"Then let's swim, damn it!" Lisa stepped closer, her gaze fierce and unwavering. "Let's swim until we reach calmer waters. Because if we don't believe our love can weather this, then what are we even doing?"

"Swimming isn't enough when you feel like you're drowning!" Oliver's anger seemed to flash as hot as the fire before them, his hands clenched at his sides.

"Is that it, then?" Lisa's throat tightened, her voice barely a whisper. "Are we drowning, Ollie? I mean, look at us; we just made love and agreed it was beautiful. We love one another."

For a moment, there was only the sound of the crashing waves and their ragged breaths. Lisa could see the struggle within Oliver, the woodworker who crafted beauty with ease yet couldn't seem to mend the fissures in his own heart.

"Sometimes, I'm scared that love isn't enough," Oliver's voice cracked, exposing a vulnerability she'd rarely seen. "Especially when I'm terrified of losing everything that matters most."

"Me too," Lisa confessed, allowing her walls to crumble. "I'm petrified. But perhaps it's that very fear that proves just how much this—how much you mean to me."

Their eyes locked, two souls stripped bare by the intensity of their own emotions… the future uncertain, yet their connection undeniable.

The wind picked up, whipping around them as if the earth itself could sense the turmoil brewing in their hearts. Lisa reached out, her fingers brushing against Oliver's, a silent plea for understanding amidst the chaos of their fears. He looked at her, his eyes a tempest of emotion, and let their hands intertwine.

The simple touch was a reminder of their bond, a lifeline as the world threatened to pull them under.

"Ollie," she said, her voice laced with the warmth that had always drawn him to her, "I don't have all the answers. But I know that every moment without you would be like a day without sun."

His thumb caressed her knuckles tenderly, and for a fleeting second, it seemed as though they were back in the safe haven of their love, protected from the storm that raged around them. But the specter of their argument lingered, an unspoken shadow that refused to be ignored.

"Lisa, I—" Oliver started, the conflict clear in his furrowed brow. He paused, struggling to find the words that could bridge the chasm that had opened between them.

"Tell me," she urged, stepping closer, desperate to reclaim the unity they once took for granted.

He exhaled sharply, his chest rising and falling with the weight of his confession. "I miss the sea, the freedom… I feel trapped, not by you, but by this life we're trying to build. It's like I'm gasping for air."

Her heart clenched at his admission, the raw honesty of it cutting deeper than any fight they'd ever had. She lifted her hand to his face, tracing the line of his jaw with a tenderness that belied her inner turmoil. "We'll find our way back to the surface," she murmured, "together."

Oliver leaned into her touch, a small, vulnerable gesture that spoke volumes. They stood there, locked in a moment of connection, but the resolution they both sought remained elusive, hovering just beyond their grasp.

"Can we?" His question hung in the air, heavy with doubt.

"Can we what?" Her voice was steady, but her pulse raced with anxiety.

"Survive this? Be the couple who makes it through the storm?"

A gust of wind tugged at Lisa's hair, and she shivered, not from the cold but from the fear of what his question implied. She wanted to scream "yes" to banish the uncertainty that clouded his eyes, but the words caught in her throat, suffocated by the reality of their struggles.

Before she could respond, the sky erupted, a sudden clap of thunder rolling overhead like an omen. Rain began to fall, light at first, then quickly growing into a deluge that soaked them and chilled them to the bone.

"Let's go inside," Oliver said, his voice barely audible over the storm's roar.

They moved together, seeking shelter from the rain, but the true storm—the one raging within them —remained unsheltered, its end as unpredictable as the path of lightning across the night sky.

As they crossed the threshold of their home, Lisa turned to Oliver, her eyes searching his for something —anything—that might hint at their future. She found nothing to calm her anxiety. Oliver's eyes were cold and distant like his heart had become.

Chapter Eight

Ava's silhouette cut a sharp contrast against the fluttering curtains of the living room window, her posture an unyielding pillar amidst the sea of tension that flooded the small space. She and Daniel came over the next day while Lisa went for a walk with Julia in the stroller, and Marianne took care of the café.

The sight of her took Oliver's breath away. She was still so incredibly beautiful it seemed impossible.

The sun draped her in its fiery glow, igniting the steely resolve in her gaze as she turned to face the door. With each step Oliver took across the threshold, his heart was beating a frantic rhythm against his chest, a symphony of anticipation for the confrontation he knew was inevitable.

"Oliver," Ava's voice quivered, betraying the storm of emotions brewing beneath her composed exterior. Though laced with anger, her words carried the tremble of vulnerability as they rose and fell in the hushed room. "I can't—I won't live like this anymore. I know I said I didn't come to cause trouble. And I truly didn't. But my feelings for you… they're still there. I want to be with you. I know I'm being selfish, but I can't help it. I want you back in my life and in Daniel's. Can't you see? When we're together, it all makes sense. The way Daniel looks at you, the warmth between us, the attraction. We're a family. You have to make a choice."

She stood rooted, arms at her sides, her knuckles whitening as she fought to keep them from shaking. The air seemed to still around them, thick with the weight of her ultimatum.

"You can't ask me to just—" Oliver began, his voice trailing off as he looked at Ava. He saw not only the woman before him but also the echo of their shared past, a ghostly presence woven into the fabric of the moment. He swallowed hard, his Adam's apple bobbing with the effort to articulate feelings that had become shards of glass in his throat.

"Choose, Oliver!" Ava insisted, her plea slicing through the quietude and reverberating off the walls. Her eyes, those piercing orbs that once held nothing but adoration for him, now blazed with the fire of betrayal and hurt. They were the same eyes that watched over Daniel as he grew, had seen too much, and had forgiven even more.

Oliver felt the pull of his old life, the salt and spray of the ocean that coursed through his veins, the pull of the new one, the warmth of Lisa's smile, and the sound of her children's laughter. And Julia. Sweet little, innocent baby Julia. The room spun ever so slightly as he struggled under the gravity of Ava's demand, the air around him charged with the raw intensity of a love that refused to be ignored and another that refused to be cast aside.

The house's very foundation seemed to hold its breath, awaiting the shattering or mending of hearts. Oliver's hands hovered, uncertain whether to reach out or withdraw, as he teetered on the precipice of a decision that would define the rest of their lives—all of their lives.

Oliver's gaze flicked from the tempest in Ava's steely blues to the bright sun outside the windows. The unspoken words hung heavy, a thick fog around his thoughts as he sought a lifeline in the turbulent sea of their emotions. His lips parted, but hesitation clung to his tongue like a stubborn barnacle.

In the kitchen, Lisa stood listening. She had come back just in time to hear the ultimatum, heart racing in her chest. Lisa's knuckles whitened against the aged oak of the counter, the wood grain pressing into her skin as if trying to ground her to the earth. Her chest heaved with the effort to keep her composure, each rise and fall an echo of the hopes and fears that battled within her soul. She watched Oliver from afar as she walked to the doorway, the lines of his face etched with conflict, and felt the very air between them crackle with the charge of impending heartache.

The silence stretched as taut as the strings of an old guitar waiting to be strummed, and in it, the small town seemed to pause—its gentle winds, its rustling leaves all holding their breath for the note that would follow. Oliver's hand reached out halfway, trembled, and fell back to his side, a silent testament to the war raging behind his furrowed brow.

Lisa's heart pitched and yawed, caught in the swell. Her eyes traced the familiar curve of Oliver's jaw, the one she had traced with her fingers on quieter nights, and she willed him to see past the maelstrom to the harbor of their shared dreams, their little family. But the memory of his laughter mingling with the children's began to fade, overshadowed by the weight of Ava's presence, a ghost ship looming on their horizon. He turned and saw her standing there, tears welling up in her eyes.

"Lisa," he began, his voice a low tremble that sought to steady itself against the intense emotions, "you and I, we've built something real, something solid like the wood I shape with my hands."

Oliver's chest rose as he inhaled the scent of pine that still clung to his shirt from the workshop. "We've created a life full of laughter, quiet nights, and small victories. It's not just about us; it's about a family."

His eyes, dark and searching, met Lisa's, seeing in them the reflection of their life together—their struggles against the ebb and flow of small-town trials, the warmth of her children's embraces, the love that had grown like wildflowers in an untended field.

Ava stood rigidly, a statue carved with lines of heartache and determination. Her eyes held a history that refused to be forgotten, a testament to the passionate and turbulent past she shared with Oliver. His words hung between them, a fragile bridge over a chasm of unspoken pain.

"Oliver, how can you stand there and speak of love and family?" Ava's voice cracked the air, sharp and laden with accusation. "What of the promises we made? The dreams we shared?" Her hand flew to her chest, pressing against the fabric of her blouse as if to quell the ache beneath. "You said you'd do life with me; you promised we would always be together, that our love would never die. And now, you anchor yourself in a safe harbor and forget everything we dreamt about?"

Oliver watched her and saw in her eyes the reflection of another time—when their hopes were intertwined, and love was so deep and forceful they'd thought it would never run out.

The room seemed to contract around them, the walls echoing with the crescendo of Ava's frustration and the whispered pleas of Oliver's heart. This was the precipice of choice, the moment where the next step would seal their fates, and in it, the thrum of life in their small town pulsed with the urgency of a heartbeat racing toward resolution.

Through the narrow gap between the kitchen door and its frame, Lisa watched with bated breath, the scene unfolding like a storm that could wash away everything she held dear. Each of Ava's words sliced through the air, tearing at the fabric of the life she had so carefully stitched together with Oliver. Her chest tightened, her pulse erratic against the steady rhythm of the grandfather clock in the corner, its ticking a metronome to the chaos.

Tears brimmed in Lisa's eyes, spilling over and tracing silent paths down her cheeks. She clung to the edge of the counter, her knuckles white, as if by sheer will she could hold onto the man she loved, keep him from being pulled back into the riptide of his past with Ava. The very thought of losing Oliver—of losing the love that had helped her through her darkest nights—sent a shiver through her.

"Please, Ava," Oliver's voice cut through the tension, a tremulous note of regret threading through the words. His hands, those strong, capable hands that had so tenderly crafted their shared dreams into reality, now reached out with an unsteady grace toward Ava. The slight tremor betrayed his inner torment, the battle raging within him.

"Can't you see?" His fingers brushed Ava's arm, a gesture that sought to bridge the gulf between them, to somehow mend the fractures with the faintest touch. "I can't undo the past, but I'm trying to do right by the present. By Lisa, by her kids… by us."

Lisa's heart hung on every syllable, each one laden with the weight of choices made and yet to be decided. The room held its breath, the only movement the quiet dance of dust motes in the slanting light that streamed through the window.

For a moment, time itself seemed to pause, teetering on the edge of revelation. The suspense twined around them, a coil waiting to snap. Would Oliver's plea soften Ava's resolve? Would his love for Lisa be enough to anchor him, or would the ghosts of what once was drag him back to a shore now foreign?

In that fraught silence, with her heart whispering pleas to the universe, Lisa stood there waiting to hear the fate of her life and her children's lives.

Ava's gaze, once like steel, melted into a sorrowful pool as it met Oliver's. Her shoulders, squared in defiance moments before, now slumped ever so slightly.

"I have noticed how you look at her," she whispered, the words floating through the room like leaves borne away by an autumn wind. "It's the same way you used to look at me."

In that admission, there was a fracture of the world they all knew—a crack that ran deep into the foundation of their shared past. The air between them hummed with the echo of memories and lost time.

The softening of Ava's expression was the subtlest shift, yet it spoke volumes—of battles fought, dreams relinquished, and the painful grace found in letting go. It was a look that knew the cost of love, that understood its immeasurable value even as it slipped through one's fingers.

Taking in the quiet resignation etched onto Ava's face, Lisa felt a surge of something fierce and protective rise within her. It was more than a mere response; it was a call to arms for the heart she had put on the line. With each step she took toward Oliver, the wooden floorboards creaked underfoot, punctuating her resolve.

"Oliver," Lisa said, her voice steady and clear, cutting through the uncertainty that veiled the room. "I love you. I love what we have, what we've built together. And I won't let it crumble—not without a fight."

Her declaration was a lighthouse guiding them back to safer shores. In those words lay not just the promise of romance but the unyielding strength of a woman who had weathered life's harshest squalls.

The suspense hung around them, tender and taut, a breath held before the plunge. There was heartbreak in this room, yes, but also a raw, undeniable hope—the kind that thrives in the small, courageous acts of choosing love again and again.

This was their precipice, the moment before the fall or flight. Would their love be the wings to carry them over the abyss, or would they tumble into its depths? The answer lay there, in the unwavering warmth of Lisa's eyes, in the steadfast tenor of her voice, and in the silent understanding that passed between them all.

Oliver stood, the lines of his face etched with conflict. The room seemed to tilt and sway like a deck beneath him. His gaze shifted from Lisa's resolute stance back to Ava, her presence a tempest that had blown in without warning, stirring up the waters of his past.

His hands hung by his sides, each finger twitching with the urge to reach out—to whom, he couldn't say. He remembered the feel of the chisel against wood, carving intricate patterns and shapes, creating something beautiful out of raw material. Now, life demanded he carve out a decision that would shape their lives in ways more profound than any piece of art he'd ever fashioned.

"Oliver," Ava whispered, her voice slicing through the veil of silence. She drew in a breath, her chest rising as if bracing against an invisible blow. "I can't stand here and pretend that my heart doesn't ache, that I don't remember every promise we made once to each other."

Her eyes, once fierce with conviction, now shimmered with unshed tears.

"I see the way you look at her—the way your world seems to orbit around Lisa, around the life you've built."

Ava's words were heavy with surrender, each syllable laden with the weight of their shared memories. "So, I'll step aside, Oliver. For you, for Daniel... I'll let you choose the life you want to live without me standing in your way. Daniel and I will leave town. You'll never see us again."

The tremble in her voice betrayed the steel of her resolve, yet it was the finality of her stance that stole the breath from his lungs. Oliver's heart, a vessel caught between two shores, felt the pull of both—Ava, the siren song of a love lost to time, and Lisa, the beacon of a future filled with promise. The room held its breath.

Lisa's breath hitched in her chest, the world around her narrowing to the echo of Ava's surrender. Her fingers, which had been white-knuckled against the cool edges of the kitchen counter earlier, now relaxed incrementally as the weight of impending loss lifted from her shoulders. The surprise that widened her eyes was mirrored by a burgeoning warmth that spread through her chest—a warmth fostered by relief and an overwhelming sense of gratitude.

"Oliver," she whispered, almost inaudible amid the tension that still hung in the air.

Oliver stood motionless, his figure a stark silhouette against the fading light of day that filtered through the window. His once poised demeanor, the embodiment of strength and resolve that Lisa had come to rely on, gave way to a vulnerability she had seldom seen. As Ava's footsteps receded, his shoulders slumped.

Lisa watched him, her heart caught between the

exhilaration of their future together and empathy for the turmoil she knew tore at his soul. With every step Ava took away from them, Oliver seemed to diminish, his frame shrinking under the burden of choices made and roads not taken. His hands, those skilled artisans of wood that had crafted their life together piece by piece, now dangled limply at his sides.

The silence that Ava left behind was profound, its presence an entity in itself, forcing Oliver and Lisa into a reality they would now have to navigate together. The love that bound them was palpable, yet so was the sorrow of sacrifice. Would Oliver resent Lisa for not being able to see his son? Would he blame her?

"Oliver?" Lisa's voice was stronger now, laced with the determination of a woman who had fought tooth and nail for the semblance of peace she'd found in this small town, in this very room, with this man whose heart had been a contested terrain.

He turned toward her slowly, his eyes carrying the glimmer of hope reignited by Ava's act. His look conveyed both the depth of his pain and the promise of healing, a silent vow that he belonged there with Lisa and her children.

"Lisa," he finally said, his voice a soft rumble filled with complexities of emotion, "I'm here."

And within those three words lay the thrilling pulse of a new chapter that promised the suspense of challenges yet to be faced and the heartwarming assurance that they would face them together.

Oliver reached out, his fingers weaving through Lisa's with a firm yet gentle grasp, conveying an unspoken pledge as they both acknowledged the turmoil that lay behind them and the rocky path that stretched ahead. They stood in silent solidarity, the weight of past choices lingering like a shadow across the room, but their clasped hands were a testament to a bond resilient enough to weather any storm.

Lisa could feel the calluses on Oliver's palms, remnants of his life at sea, and the strength within his grip that had so often been her anchor. His touch was steady and reassuring, promising that together, they would navigate the unpredictable tides of their small-town existence.

The room hummed with tension still dissipating, yet a newfound electricity was in the air, a current charged with hope and possibility. The walls, once mere witnesses to their strife, now seemed to lean in closer, eager to absorb the warmth radiating from the couple at its center.

"Whatever comes next," Lisa said, her voice low but unwavering, "we'll face it. We can do it."

Oliver nodded, his eyes locking with hers, a silent storm of emotions swirling within their depths.

"Always," he replied, the simple word heavy with conviction. "And forever."

Outside, the first drops of rain began to fall against the windowpane, a prelude to the tempest brewing on the horizon. But inside, cradled within the four walls of the home they had built from love and shared dreams, Lisa and Oliver stood united. Their intertwined hands were not just an emblem of their union but a symbol of courage in the face of the unknowns that awaited them.

As they turned to look out the window, watching the sky darken and the wind pick up, neither flinched. Instead, they found solace in the rhythmic patter of the rain, a drumbeat to which they would set their dance into the future—a dance made all the more exhilarating by the certainty that they would step through it in unison, their hearts beating as one.

Never could they have known at this point what darkness awaited them.

Chapter Nine

The bell above the café door jingled, its quaint chime belying the tension that trailed in with Ava and her son Daniel. Lisa, wiping down a table, looked up and was surprised to see Ava's eyes, usually as clear and calm as a summer sky, now clouded with the remnants of tears. Lisa's heart sank.

What are they doing here? Did she regret her decision? Has she come back for Oliver after all?

The little boy's hand was engulfed in his mother's firm grip, his mop of dark hair bouncing with each step they took toward the counter.

"Ava? I thought you left town?" Lisa called out softly. Seeing the look on their faces, her maternal instincts kicked into high gear as she tucked the cleaning cloth into her apron and approached them. "Why don't you come on back? Let's go upstairs for a bit."

Ava gave a slight nod, relief momentarily flickering across her features. She allowed Lisa to lead them through the kitchen and up the narrow stairs to the cozy apartment above the café. The smell of roasted coffee beans followed them, a comforting aroma that felt at odds with the palpable unease Ava carried like a shawl around her shoulders.

Once seated at the small kitchen table, Lisa poured two mugs of coffee and one with chocolate milk for Daniel, who swung his legs idly under the chair. Ava's resolve seemed to rebuild between sips of the steamy brew, the steel in her spine becoming more apparent.

"Lisa, I need to talk to Oliver," Ava said, and the gravity in her voice pulled at Lisa's heartstrings. "It's important."

"Sure, Ava," Lisa replied, her mind spinning with possibilities, each more troubling than the last. What could be so urgent that it would bring Ava here, unannounced, with such a haunted look in her eyes? As she waited for Oliver to return from the woodshop, her hands twisted the edge of her apron, an outward sign of the turmoil brewing within.

Time stretched thin until, finally, the front door creaked open. Oliver's tall frame filled the doorway, his dark hair tousled from a day spent working with his hands. His expression shifted from casual cheer to concern as he spotted Ava and Daniel, an unspoken question hanging between them like a heavy curtain.

"Oliver," Ava stood up, clasping Daniel's hand again.

"Hey, what's—?" But Oliver's greeting was cut short by the sheer urgency etched into Ava's face, and his eyes darted to Lisa for explanation.

Lisa remained silent, her gaze locked on Oliver. She could hear her heartbeat, a relentless drum against her ribcage, as she watched him navigate the unexpected encounter. Every muscle in her body tensed, preparing for the unknown as if bracing for the aftershock of an earthquake.

"Let's sit down," Oliver suggested after a moment, his voice steady but his eyes betraying a flicker of anxiety. He pulled out chairs for Ava and Daniel and settled across from them, his hands resting on the table in a gesture of openness.

"Alright, Ava," he said, the timber of his voice soft yet firm. "Tell me what's going on."

As the scene unfolded before her, Lisa clutched the mug in her hands, the warmth from the coffee seeping into her skin but doing nothing to thaw the chill of apprehension that had settled deep in her bones. The path ahead was shrouded in mystery, and with every passing second, the homey atmosphere grew thick with suspense, the weight of hidden truths yet to be unveiled.

Ava's fingers danced nervously on the edge of the table, her eyes flitting between Oliver and the steaming mug before her as if searching for the right words in the wisps of vapor. The room seemed to hold its breath, the quiet only disturbed by the soft patter of rain against the windowpane.

"Oliver," she began, her voice barely more than a

whisper, betraying the turmoil beneath her composed exterior. "There's something I need to tell you. It's about why I'm here." She paused, gathering the shards of her resolve. "It's not just a visit. It's not just so you can get to know Daniel."

Lisa watched from the periphery, her hands now still. The earlier warmth of the coffee was replaced by a cold knot of fear coiling in her stomach.

"I've been… involved in something," Ava continued, her gaze locking onto Oliver's, pleading silently for understanding. "Someone… someone is after me. And Daniel." Her breath hitched, her son's name evoking a protective fierceness in her eyes. "We had to get away. We needed a safe place to hide."

The revelation hung in the air, dense and heavy. Oliver's face, moments ago etched with concern, now mirrored the shock that reverberated through Lisa's entire being. His brow furrowed deeply as he leaned back in his chair, the wood creaking under the shift of his weight. Disbelief and worry blended into a silent storm in his dark eyes.

"God, Ava…" Oliver's voice broke the spell of stunned silence. He ran a hand through his tousled hair, struggling to reconcile the woman who once held his heart with the frightened figure before him. With each breath, he fought through the haze of emotions —a maelstrom of affection for Lisa, gnawing dread for Ava's plight, and an undeniable pull toward the young boy with eyes so much like his own. "What kind of danger are we talking about? What have you done?"

"I... I can't get into the details. It's better if you don't know," she said.

"Are you saying you're both in danger right now? Here?" Oliver's question was firm, demanding that reality assert itself amidst the chaos of thoughts vying for attention in his mind.

Ava nodded, clasping Daniel's hand tighter as though anchoring herself to the present moment. "Yes, that's exactly what I'm saying. We are in danger —immediate danger."

The words seemed to echo, bouncing off the walls and settling heavily around them. Oliver's chest rose and fell with a deep, steadying breath as he grappled with the gravity of the situation. There was a decision lurking on the horizon, one that would test the very fabric of their lives. A choice between the love he knew and the responsibility that now demanded his embrace.

"I can't believe you, Ava. I can't believe this. I need to..." Oliver finally said, the words cutting through the tension. "I need to take a walk to think about this."

As a spectator of the unraveling drama, Lisa felt her pulse quicken at his proclamation. The stakes were higher than ever, and as the storm outside whispered promises of uncertainty, their home became an unlikely fortress against the tempest brewing beyond its doors.

A delicate chime resonated through the café as a gust of wind announced Oliver's leaving, but the sound was lost under the weight of Ava's confession. Lisa, her heart thundering against her ribs, watched as the room's atmosphere thickened with tension. She could see the fear etched into Ava's face, the tremble in her lips, and something within Lisa shifted. The cold grip of shock that had seized her heart melted away, replaced by a warm current of empathy.

"Sweetheart," Lisa said, her voice soft but resolute. She reached across the divide of uncertainty to touch Ava's arm lightly. "We'll make it right, somehow."

Ava's eyes, brimming with gratitude, met Lisa's. They were windows to a soul that had seen too much, yet they shone with an unspoken plea for sanctuary. Lisa's own struggles, the nights spent staring at the ceiling, wondering if she'd ever feel safe again, echoed back at her in those blue depths. She understood—the fear, the desperation, the fierce instinct to protect one's child. It bound them together despite the chaos swirling around them.

At Ava's side, Daniel stood like a small sentinel, his young face pinched with confusion. His grip on Ava's hand was a silent testament to his anxiety, the only thing he knew to do in a world that suddenly seemed too large and menacing. Lisa's gaze softened as she looked down at him, her maternal instincts kicking in.

"Hey, buddy," she coaxed gently, bending slightly to be at his eye level. Daniel's gaze flickered up to meet hers, searching for some semblance of understanding amid the storm of adult emotions. Lisa offered him a reassuring smile, her fingers brushing over his knotted curls in a comforting gesture. "You're safe here, Daniel. You're with family."

Still uncertain but visibly calmed by her touch, Daniel managed a tentative smile in return, the innocence in his eyes striking a chord in Lisa's chest. At that moment, any remnants of doubt about what needed to be done dissipated. This wasn't just about old flames and complicated pasts; this was about a mother and her child seeking refuge from a threat that had chased them into the arms of this quiet town.

The café, with its homely aroma of coffee and the familiar creak of its wooden floors, had always been a place of comfort for Lisa. Now, it took on a new role—a haven for those with nowhere else to turn. As the rain lashed against the windows, promising a storm that mirrored their inner turmoil, Lisa felt a steely resolve settle within her. They would face this together, and she would fight with every fiber of her being to keep this newfound family intact.

Oliver's hand hesitated on the doorknob. With a quiet click, he entered the dimly lit hallway of the home he shared with Lisa, the sound of rain a steady thrum against the window panes. He found Ava, her silhouette etched with both strength and vulnerability in the soft glow of the living room lamp.

"Oliver," she whispered, her voice carrying the

weight of a thousand unspoken words. "I'm sorry. I wouldn't have come here if it wasn't important."

"I thought you came here for me—because you wanted to be with me and for me to get to know our son. But of course not. How could I have been so blind?"

"I did come here for you," she said. "And for Daniel."

He could see the lines of worry creasing her forehead and Daniel's restless shuffle at her side. The boy's eyes held a silent plea that echoed in Oliver's chest. In that gaze, he saw the bridge between his present and a past that had suddenly resurfaced, as tangible as the salty air he used to breathe on the fishing boat before the world he knew was distilled into the fine grains of sawdust in his workshop.

"Hey, buddy," Oliver said softly to Daniel, offering a small but genuine smile that belied the violent emotions brewing within him. He crouched down to the boy's level, seeking the solace of innocence in a situation far too complex.

As he stood up, his eyes met Lisa's, and he found an anchor in them. Her presence was the calm in his tempest, her resilience something that had subtly woven itself into his very being. But now, with Ava's confession, the threads of his life felt frayed and tangled. What kind of danger was she involved in? Why had she brought that to him? And into Daniel's life? He couldn't believe her. She was supposed to protect the boy.

"Oliver…" Lisa began, her tone a soothing balm, "I know this is hard for you."

He drew a deep breath, the reality settling upon him like the heavy coastal fog. A decision loomed, its shadow darkening the space between him and the two women who stood before him, each holding a piece of his heart.

"Lisa, I—" His voice cracked, the words lodged in his throat as he tried to navigate the maelstrom of love and duty.

"Oliver," Lisa cut in, her eyes never leaving his, "Ava's in trouble. We can't turn our backs on her or Daniel." Her voice was firm yet threaded with warmth, the embodiment of the compassion that made her who she was.

"I know," Oliver replied, the struggle evident in the tightness of his jaw. "It's just… it's a lot."

"Of course it is," Lisa said, stepping closer. She reached out, her hand finding his, their fingers intertwining in a silent vow of solidarity. "But we're in this together. Whatever needs to be done to keep Ava and Daniel safe, we'll make it happen."

Her conviction stirred something within him, a spark of hope amidst the chaos. It was not just a promise to Ava but a testament to the life he and Lisa had built—one that could weather any storm, even those that blew in unexpectedly, threatening to upend everything.

"Thank you," Ava breathed out, her eyes glistening with unshed tears, reflecting the depth of her gratitude and the harrowing journey that had led her here. "Thank you both."

The room seemed to hold its breath, the three adults and one child bound by a complicated tapestry of emotions and histories. And yet, amid it all, there was an undeniable sense of unity—a resolve to protect, shelter, and stand as one against whatever perils lay beyond the walls of the cozy café turned sanctuary.

Oliver stood by the window, the late afternoon sun casting long shadows across the room. Daniel played quietly in the corner, his toy cars making soft rumbling sounds on the hardwood floor. The child's innocence was a stark contrast to the weighty silence that had settled among the adults. Oliver turned from the window, his gaze locking onto Ava's.

"Look at me, Ava," he said, the timbre of his voice steady and sure. "No matter what happens next, I will always be here for Daniel. He's part of my life now, and I won't turn my back on him. I want you both to stay here with us and not at the inn anymore." His words were a light in the storm, his resolve shining through despite the uncertainty ahead.

Ava nodded, her lips quivering as she attempted to speak. "Thank you, Oliver," she finally managed, her voice a mere whisper but imbued with relief.

Lisa watched the exchange, her heart swelling with a mix of pride and trepidation. She knew Oliver's promise was not just to Ava but also to herself and the future they hoped to build. Lisa approached Oliver, her steps hesitant yet purposeful.

"Oliver," she began, her voice a mixture of warmth and worry, "we need to talk about how this changes things for us."

He turned to face her, his dark eyes searching hers for understanding. "I know, Lisa. Everything feels like it's hanging by a thread, doesn't it?" His hands found hers, their fingers entwining much like roots seeking stability in the earth.

"More than ever," she admitted, squeezing his hands as if to anchor herself to the moment. "But whatever comes our way, we face it together—you and me. We've been through tough times before, and we've come out stronger." Her words carried the weight of their shared history, the battles they had fought side by side.

"Stronger, yes," Oliver agreed, a half-smile tugging at the corners of his mouth. His woodworker's hands, rough and calloused, were gentle as they cradled her face. "We have to stay united, not just for Daniel, but for us."

Lisa felt a shiver of anticipation run through her. The road ahead was fraught with unknowns, yet the steadfast love she saw in Oliver's eyes steeled her. "I'm scared," she confessed, allowing vulnerability to seep into her usually resilient façade. "But with you, I feel like we can handle anything—even this mess."

"I'm worried too. And scared, I guess. Scared is good sometimes," Oliver whispered, leaning in to rest his forehead against hers. "It means we're alive and fighting for something worth holding onto."

"Whatever happens," Oliver said, pulling back just enough to look into Lisa's eyes, "I am committed to you, to us. To the life we're trying to build together."

And with those words, the threads of their lives—tangled, frayed, yet unbroken—wove tighter still, forming a tapestry rich with love, courage, and the unyielding human spirit.

Ava's hands trembled as she lifted the steaming mug to her lips, the aroma of dark coffee unable to mask the thick tension in the room. She set the cup down with a clink that seemed too loud in the hushed space of Lisa's cozy kitchen. Her eyes, usually so fierce, now brimmed with unshed tears that reflected both gratitude and pain.

"Lisa, Oliver," Ava began, her voice wavering but resolute, "I can't ever repay you for this—your kindness, the sanctuary you've offered. But I have thought it over, and I can't accept it. I can't stay here with you and be a burden. It will put all of you and your children in danger. I can't do that to you. I know leaving is the only way to keep you all safe. It's just..." She paused, her gaze drifting to where Daniel played quietly on the rug, his toy cars zipping along an imaginary highway, blissfully unaware of the gravity surrounding him.

Oliver reached out, his hand finding Ava's shoulder in a reassuring squeeze.

"It's going to be okay, Ava," Lisa said, her voice carrying the warmth of her smile even as it quivered with emotion and uncertainty. She moved closer, bridging the gap between them, her presence a silent vow of support. "We will take care of him."

The words hung in the air, heavy with promise and sacrifice. Daniel looked up then, his little face scrunched in concentration as he tried to grasp the undercurrents of the adult conversation. He toddled over, sensing the need for closeness, and Lisa scooped him into her arms. His innocent laughter was a poignant reminder of what was at stake.

"Thank you," Ava whispered, her eyes locked on her son, the love there as fierce as a storm. "I trust you both with everything that I am. With Daniel." Her resolve flickered like a candle in the wind, but the flame held strong. "Please, give him the life I can't right now—a life without fear, filled with love."

"We will," Oliver assured her, his voice steady despite the maelstrom of emotions he wrestled within. "He's my blood, Ava. I'll protect him with my life."

In that moment, the three adults formed an unspoken pact, their shared commitment to Daniel transcending the chaos of their past and the uncertainty of the future. As they stood in the soft glow of the kitchen light, surrounded by the scent of freshly brewed coffee and the sound of a child's contented sighs, the outside world—with its danger and dark secrets—faded to mere shadows at the edge of their haven.

Lisa glanced at Oliver, her partner in every sense, and felt their bond deepen. They were embarking on a journey neither had anticipated, but together, they would navigate the perils. Their love was a compass in the wilds; their courage, the sails to weather any storm. And though the road ahead was shrouded in mystery, they knew one thing for certain: they would face whatever came with unity and an unwavering determination to protect their newfound family.

Ava's silhouette framed the doorway, her figure poised on the threshold of departure. The late afternoon sun cast a warm glow on her face, an interplay of light and shadow that reflected the turmoil within her heart. She clutched a small, well-worn duffel bag with one hand while the other lingered on the doorframe as if to anchor herself a moment longer in the life she was about to leave behind.

Lisa watched from across the room, where she stood enveloped in Oliver's embrace. His arms were wrapped around her, strong and sure, yet gentle—a fortress in human form. Lisa leaned into his chest, her ear pressed against the steady rhythm of his heartbeat. It was a sound that spoke of constancy and comfort, a balm to the chaos that churned just beneath the surface of their lives.

"Hey," Oliver whispered, tilting Lisa's chin up to

meet his gaze. His eyes, dark and fathomless, held a promise that transcended words. He brushed a stray wavy lock from her forehead, tucking it gently behind her ear. "We're in this together, remember? No matter what happens."

Lisa nodded, a lump forming in her throat. The weight of their decision pressed down on her, but Oliver's presence was a buoy keeping her afloat. "Together," she echoed, the word a lifeline between them.

Oliver kissed her then, a soft press of lips that sealed their vow. It was a kiss filled with the layers of their shared history—the trials they'd overcome and the love that had blossomed from adversity. In that brief communion, they reaffirmed their commitment to each other and the new path they were forging.

The tender moment was broken by the faint rustle of Ava shifting from foot to foot, a reminder of the farewell that loomed over them. Lisa released a slow breath and stepped back from Oliver's hold, turning to face Ava with resolve etched into her features.

"Take care of yourself, Ava," Lisa said, her voice thick with unshed tears. "And know that Daniel will always have a home here with us."

Ava nodded, her eyes brimming with a complex cocktail of emotions. Gratitude warred with grief, and hope sparred with heartache.

"Thank you, both of you. I—I won't forget this." Her words faltered, strained by the gravity of goodbye.

Oliver crossed the distance to Ava, his movements

hesitant yet compelled by a force stronger than reluctance. He enveloped her in a brief, tight hug, the kind that tried to bridge the gap of years and the chasm of circumstance in a single gesture. When he pulled away, his jaw was set, a muscle ticking in a silent struggle.

"Be safe," he murmured, his voice barely above a whisper. It shattered something inside Lisa to witness his pain, knowing that part of his heart would always belong to Ava and the life they might have had.

With a final glance laden with unsaid words and unshed tears, Ava turned and stepped out into the fading light of day. The door closed softly behind her, its click resounding like the closing of a book—one chapter ending so another could begin.

Lisa reached for Oliver's hand, lacing her fingers through his as they moved toward the window. They watched in silence as Ava's figure receded down the dusty road, her steps carrying her away from them, from the town, from the threat that drove her into hiding.

"Will she be alright?" Lisa asked, the question hanging between them tinged with worry and wonder.

Oliver squeezed her hand, his gaze never leaving the retreating figure. "She's survived this long; she's stronger than we know. And we'll be here… for Daniel and each other."

The sun dipped below the horizon, painting the sky in shades of fiery orange and calming purple—a canvas of endings and beginnings. As darkness crept over the landscape, Lisa and Oliver remained at the window, united in their silent vigil, hearts bound by love and a fierce determination to face whatever lay ahead.

The first star of the evening blinked into existence as Lisa and Oliver's eyes lingered on the empty road where Ava had disappeared. The cool night breeze whispered through the open window, carrying a chill that seemed to echo the uncertainty now settling in their hearts.

"Oliver," Lisa murmured, her voice barely above the rustle of leaves outside. "If she was running from something or someone, does that mean they could come here? Looking for her… for Daniel?"

Oliver pulled away from the window, his features etched with lines of concern in the fading light. He wrapped his arm around Lisa, ushering her away from the view of the darkening road.

"I don't know," he admitted, the weight of his admission pressing down on them both. "But we can't live in fear. We have to be smart and cautious."

Lisa nodded, finding solace in the strength of his embrace. She glanced at Daniel, who sat on the living room floor, his small fingers playing with a toy airplane, oblivious to the gravity of the adults' conversation.

"Let's not let these shadows dim the home we've built," Lisa said with a resolve that surprised even herself. "We'll keep him safe together. And if trouble comes knocking…."

"Then we'll face it like we do everything else," Oliver finished for her, his voice resolute. "With love, and if necessary, with the fiercest protection we can muster."

"Tomorrow," Lisa spoke with a newfound determination, "we'll put new locks on the doors, check in with Sheriff Coleman, and maybe get a security system installed."

"First thing in the morning," Oliver agreed, his hand finding hers again, their fingers interlocking with silent promises of mutual support.

They both knew sleep would not come easily tonight, but there was a sense of unity between them—a bond forged in the fires of shared adversity.

Chapter Ten

The crackling fire in the hearth cast a soft glow over the living room, where Lisa and Oliver lounged on the couch, lost in each other's company—the quiet evening wrapped around them like a comforting blanket. Her wavy brown hair fell gently around her shoulders as she tilted her head back against the couch, laughing at something Oliver had just said.

"Life's pretty good, isn't it?" Oliver mused, his eyes reflecting the flames, a contented smile playing on his lips. His hand found Lisa's.

"It is," Lisa agreed, her voice a warm murmur. She savored these moments of peace, knowing all too well how fleeting they could be. Her gaze lingered on Oliver, appreciating not only the rugged handsomeness that first drew her to him but also the steadfast support he'd become for her and the children.

Their tranquility shattered with the jarring ring of his phone. Lisa's heart skipped a beat, an old reflex from darker times. Oliver answered, his body tensing as he listened, the relaxed air around him evaporating instantaneously.

"Oliver, it's me—Ava," came the ragged, breathless voice on the other end. "I—I'm in trouble. They've found me." Panic threaded through her words, her fear palpable even through the phone.

"Slow down, Ava. What's happened?" Despite the alarming news, Oliver's voice was steady, a rock amidst the swirling tide of distress.

"I thought I could leave before they caught up, but it's too late. Please, you have to protect Daniel!" Ava's plea sliced through the room, her desperation striking Oliver straight in the heart.

"Of course, Ava, Daniel is safe with us. We'll come to you. Where are you?" Oliver's calm demeanor belied the urgency of their situation.

Lisa rose from the couch, her maternal instincts kicking into high gear as she thought of little Daniel asleep in the next room, unaware of the danger his mother faced. The boy with the messy dark hair and laughter that echoed joyfully through their home— how could she not protect him?

"Okay, Ava, stay hidden. We're on our way," Oliver assured her, ending the call. He met Lisa's worried eyes, his own reflecting the gravity of what they were about to do.

Without a word, they sprang into action. Lisa's mind raced as she considered their options. Fear gnawed at her, but she forced it down, drawing on the resilience that had carried her through her tumultuous past. She focused on the task at hand—ensuring Ava and Daniel's safety.

"Oliver, we need to be smart about this," Lisa said, her voice firm. "You know the area better than anyone; think there's a route we can take to get to Ava without being seen?"

"Back roads," Oliver replied, already grabbing his coat. "It'll take longer, but we'll avoid any main streets."

"Good," Lisa nodded, her thoughts shifting into strategic mode. The family business might be struggling, but this was no time to dwell on financial pressures. Lives were at stake.

"Take the truck. It's less conspicuous than the car, and we might need the four-wheel-drive," she added, already running through self-defense maneuvers in her mind, something she had been a little too accustomed to in her previous life with her ex-husband.

Lisa's fingers trembled as she dialed Maggie's number, the screen of her phone glowing like a guiding light in the dimly lit kitchen. "Maggie, it's Lisa. I need you to come over right away," she said, her voice barely above a whisper, every word laced with urgency.

"Lisa? What's wrong?" came the immediate response, Maggie's tone alert and ready for action.

"It's Ava. She's in trouble, and we have to help her. Can you watch the kids?"

"Of course, I'll be right there." There was no hesitation in Maggie's reply, just the steadfast solidarity that had always been her way.

"Thank you," Lisa breathed out, a shard of relief piercing through the tight coil of fear in her chest. She ended the call and slipped the phone into her pocket, turning to find Oliver by the safe, his back to her, shoulders set in grim determination.

The soft click of the safe echoed too loudly in the quiet room as Oliver retrieved his gun, the metallic glint sending a shiver down Lisa's spine. Her heart skipped a beat, not from romance but from the cold touch of dread.

"Oliver…" Her voice cracked, betraying her anxiety.

He turned, the gun now securely holstered at his side.

"I know you got that after the encounter with my ex-husband last year," Lisa said. "But that thing just scares me.

"It's just for protection, Lisa," he assured her, his eyes meeting hers. He tried to offer a smile, but it didn't reach his eyes.

"Seeing you with that… it scares me," she admitted, hugging herself tightly as if to ward off the chilling thoughts that raced through her mind.

"Hey," Oliver stepped closer, reaching out to gently cup her face with his callused hands, the hands of a man who'd crafted their life together with love and woodwork. "I won't let anything bad happen to us, to Ava, to the kids. You trust me, right?"

Lisa nodded despite the knot of worry tightening in her gut. She trusted him more than anyone, but sometimes, love wasn't a shield against bullets.

"I hear Maggie downstairs. We'll let her in, and then, let's go," she said, steeling herself with the resilience that had carried her through the toughest storms of her life.

"Remember, stay behind me once we get there," Oliver instructed, a protective edge to his voice. It was a reminder of the reality they were stepping into—a reality where being outnumbered and outgunned was a possibility they couldn't ignore. Oliver wanted her to stay home, but she needed to be at his side. It was non-negotiable.

"Always," Lisa replied, knowing full well she'd do whatever it took to keep their family safe, even if it meant facing her deepest fears head-on.

Together, they stepped outside, the night air crisp and biting, carrying the scent of impending snow. The world around them lay still, oblivious to the storm about to unfold. Hand in hand, they walked toward the truck parked in the shadow of the towering pines, the sanctuary of their home fading into the darkness behind them.

The truck's engine roared to life, echoing through the stillness as Oliver slammed his foot against the pedal. Gravel spewed behind them, a stark contrast to the looming silence that blanketed the small town. Lisa's pulse thrummed in her ears, a rhythmic reminder of the urgency driving their every move. They were racing against time—against fate and the unknown dangers lurking in the shadows.

Oliver navigated the winding roads with an intensity that matched Lisa's tight grip on the door handle. His eyes, usually warm and inviting, were now sharp with focus, darting back and forth as if trying to predict what lay ahead. She could almost feel the weight of the gun he had secured on his side, a cold, unfamiliar presence that sent shivers down her spine despite the warmth of the heater.

"Almost there," Oliver murmured, more to himself than to her.

Lisa nodded, not trusting her voice amidst the torrent of fears swirling inside her. She thought of Ava and Daniel—the little boy who had become like one of her own—and let those thoughts fuel her courage.

As they approached Ava's hiding place, a rickety cabin tucked away at the edge of town, the sight of its dimly lit windows gave hope but also served as a signal of potential peril. Oliver killed the headlights and coasted the last few yards, bringing the vehicle to a silent stop.

"Stay close," he whispered, his hand finding hers as they exited the truck, their boots crunching softly on the frost-coated grass. Lisa's heart felt as if it were trying to escape her chest, but she clung to Oliver's steadying presence, allowing it to anchor her.

Inside, they found Ava huddled in a corner, her once vibrant eyes clouded with terror. At the sight of them, a faint glimmer sparked momentarily before being swallowed by the darkness of her fear.

"Lisa… Oliver…" Ava's voice was a frail whisper lost in the vastness of her despair.

"Shh, we're here now, Ava," Lisa soothed, kneeling beside her and enveloping her in an embrace that promised safety and unwavering support. We'll get you through this."

Oliver stood guard by the door, his gaze vigilant, but his expression softened as he watched Lisa cradle Ava's trembling form. It was a testament to the strength of their bond, forged through shared adversity and the unspoken vows of protection they had made to each other.

"Everything's going to be okay," Lisa reassured her, though the words were as much for herself as they were for Ava. The night outside was holding its breath, waiting for their next move, while inside the cabin, three hearts beat in unison—a symphony of hope amidst the chaos.

Oliver's hand slipped into Lisa's as they peered through the crack in the aged curtains. The moonlight revealed a creeping malice outside, where shadows moved with sinister purpose.

"They're here. Looks like there's four… no, five of them," Oliver whispered, his voice a low rumble of contained urgency. Their breaths fogged the glass, mingling in the cold air that seemed to seep through every crevice of the worn cabin.

Lisa's mind raced, her heart a drumbeat echoing

the pulse of danger that throbbed just beyond the walls. They were few, their foes many, and the biting Alaskan chill was no ally tonight. She knew the gun Oliver had secured was a mere whisper of defiance against the cacophony of threats surrounding them.

"Stay down, Ava," Lisa instructed, her tone firm yet threaded with an undercurrent of warmth. "Keep Daniel in your thoughts—that's your job now. Ours is to lead them away."

Ava nodded, her eyes a pair of blue flames flickering with trust in the dim light. Lisa squeezed her shoulder, an unspoken vow passing between them. She stood, her resolve crystallizing into action.

"Oliver," she said. "We can do this."

"Right." He nodded, his determination a match for hers. Together, they mapped out their plan in hushed tones—a dance of strategy where each step could mean salvation or peril.

"Ready?" he murmured, the door handle cold under his touch.

"Always," Lisa replied, her wavy brown hair a cascade of shadows as she turned, poised to burst forth into the night.

Together, they flung open the door, charging into the frigid embrace of the outside world. Every footfall was a defiant drum against the earth, every breath a battle cry. They darted through the trees, hearts ablaze with the fire of their love—for each other, for Ava, for the life they'd built.

Behind them, the cabin remained a silent sentinel, guarding its precious secret. Inside, Ava's form melded into the darkness, her presence an undetectable whisper amongst the creaks and sighs of the aging timber.

The chase had begun, but Lisa and Oliver carried within them the unyielding spirit of the small town—a bastion of hope that would not easily be extinguished. Together, they ran, their love an unbreakable chain that bound them to each other and the promise of a future free from fear.

Oliver's breath formed ghostly plumes in the frigid air as he led their pursuers through a labyrinth of snow-laden trees. His boots, familiar with the uneven terrain of the Alaskan wilderness, found purchase on hidden roots and stones that would send an unfamiliar man sprawling. Lisa's shadow flitted just behind him, her frame agile despite the icy fingers of fear that clawed at her heart.

"Through here," Oliver hissed, veering sharply to the left where the forest grew denser. He remembered this part of the woods from his younger days when he wandered off the beaten paths in search of tranquility.

Branches snagged at Lisa's hair, pulling wavy strands free from her hurried ponytail, yet she moved undeterred. They could hear the crunching steps and muffled curses of the men behind them—a discordant symphony to their own desperate rhythm.

"Oliver, now!" Lisa called out, recognizing the sign they had agreed upon earlier—a gnarled tree, standing sentinel-like amidst its brethren, marking the spot where they'd split.

With a nod, they parted ways momentarily. Oliver continued the chase, leading the men further into the wild with the promise of capture, while Lisa doubled back, circling around with the stealth of a seasoned predator.

Her heart pounded in her chest, a drumbeat urging her forward as she positioned herself behind a thick stand of shrubbery. She crouched low, senses heightened, waiting for the moment to strike. A solitary figure appeared, slightly distanced from the rest, his attention fixed on following Oliver's tracks. This was the man she would take down.

As he neared her hiding place, oblivious to the trap laid before him, Lisa sprang into action. Her movements were fluid—those of a mother who had transformed her fear into fortitude, her caution into combativeness. She remembered the self-defense classes taken after leaving her troubled marriage, never imagining they'd serve her in such a life-or-death context.

She caught the man by surprise, her forearm colliding with his throat, cutting off his air. As he staggered, she swept his legs from under him, sending him crumpling to the snow. His weapon skittered away, useless. With swift efficiency, she delivered a disabling blow to his temple, ensuring he wouldn't rise anytime soon.

"Stay down," she warned, though her words were

unnecessary—the man was out cold, a silent testament to Lisa's resolve.

Oliver's breath came out in clouds, visible in the sharp Alaskan air, as he reached the ridge where Lisa was crouched. The moonlight cast an ethereal glow on her wavy brown hair, now damp with sweat from the exertion. Their eyes met for a fleeting moment, the unspoken fear and determination passing between them like an electric current.

"Are you okay?" Oliver whispered, his voice rough with concern. "I lost them, I think."

Lisa nodded, her breaths coming in short bursts that matched the erratic pounding of her heart. "We can't keep running," she said, the icy wind carrying her words away almost as quickly as they were spoken. "They'll just come after us again. We have to end this."

Her fingers brushed against his, a silent promise of solidarity. The smell of pine and earth filled their senses, grounding them amidst the chaos.

"Let's use the old cannery," Oliver suggested, the gears in his mind turning as he envisioned their escape. "No one goes there anymore since it shut down. It's full of hiding spots, and we know every inch of it."

Lisa's eyes lit up with the spark of strategy. "We can make it look like we're cornered," she added, piecing together the plan. "And when they move in...."

"We take them by surprise," Oliver finished for her, the corners of his lips tilting up in a grim smile. "There are plenty of tools left behind we can use as weapons. And the upper walkways—they won't expect an attack from above."

"Exactly." Lisa's reply was firm, her resilient spirit shining through despite the tremors of adrenaline that coursed through her veins. She had faced darkness before and would face it again, not just for herself but for Ava, Daniel, and all her children.

"Let's go, then," Oliver said, extending his hand to help her up. They moved swiftly, their footsteps nearly silent on the forest floor as they made their way toward the shadowy silhouette of the cannery looming in the distance.

As they approached the derelict structure, Oliver's knowledge of the town's hidden spots became their greatest asset. They slipped through an opening in the fence that time and neglect had hidden from casual observers. Inside, the musty scent of old fish and rust assaulted their nostrils, an olfactory relic of prosperous times long gone.

"Remember, stay quiet and hidden until the right moment," Lisa instructed, her voice barely above a whisper as they split up to cover more ground.

"Always," Oliver replied, his dark eyes reflecting the steel within him.

With its labyrinthine corridors and secret alcoves, the cannery offered a haunting backdrop for their high-stakes game of cat and mouse. Lisa felt a kinship with the shadows as she melded into them, her presence as imperceptible as the ghosts that some claimed still haunted the place.

Time seemed to stretch and compress in odd ways as they waited in ambush. Each second was a drumbeat of anticipation, each minute a lifetime of hope and fear intertwined.

The trap was set, and now all that was left was for their pursuers to step right into it.

Oliver's figure darted between the rusting equipment and stacks of wooden pallets, his movements a silent dance in the dim light. Lisa crouched behind a corroded old conveyor belt, her breath steady despite the thunderous pulse in her ears. Dust motes danced in the slivers of light that pierced the gloom, each particle charged with the electricity of their peril.

The trap was simple yet ingenious—a network of tripwires connected to a cacophony of metal cans and tools, poised to create a diversion. The pursuers, they hoped, would be drawn by the noise, allowing Lisa and Oliver to circle behind them.

A sudden crash echoed through the cannery, the sound of their plan springing to life. Lisa's heart leaped into her throat. She exchanged a glance with Oliver from across the room; it was time.

"Go!" she mouthed, and they surged forward.

Lisa's muscles coiled and released as she sprinted, her once cautious trust now an unbreakable bond with Oliver, who moved like a shadow a few feet beside her.

They rounded a corner, and there they were—two figures caught off-guard, searching for the source of the clamor. Oliver's hand found Lisa's, a fleeting touch that conveyed years of unspoken promises. Then, with the grace of the fisherman he once was, he cast a length of heavy netting he had salvaged, ensnaring one of the men.

"Lisa!" Oliver shouted, a rare break in his composure as the second man turned on him.

Time seemed to fracture, seconds splintering into moments of raw terror and fierce determination. Lisa sprang into action, her body moving with the self-defense techniques drilled into muscle memory.

"Back off!" she yelled, her voice slicing through the tense air. Her leg shot out, connecting with her assailant's knee in a perfect arc. He stumbled, giving her the opening to drive her elbow into his solar plexus.

The man crumpled, gasping for air, but Lisa didn't pause to watch. She was already at Oliver's side, helping to subdue the trapped pursuer, when someone sprang at him from the shadows. Lisa watched as Oliver tumbled to the floor with a thud.

"Oliver!"

Lisa's arms ached, her grip tightening on a heavy metal pipe she had snagged from the floor. Oliver was locked in a struggle with the larger of their pursuers, his face set in grim determination. The man's relentless advances seemed like a mountain pressing down upon them, and Lisa felt the ice of fear creeping into her veins.

"Oliver!" she cried out, swinging the pipe with all her might. It connected with a dull thud against the attacker's side, causing him to grunt in pain and stagger away from Oliver.

Oliver seized the moment, his fisherman's strength honed from years at sea surging through him. He lunged forward, his fist connecting with the man's jaw, sending him tumbling to the ground.

"Stay down!" Oliver commanded, his voice a rumble of thunder in the eerie calm that followed.

With the immediate threat neutralized, they turned to each other, their chests heaving in unison. A wave of relief washed over Lisa, the same kind that came after a storm when the sea lay still and forgiving once more. Their eyes met, and in Oliver's gaze, she saw not just the shared victory but also the echo of every challenge they had overcome together.

"Come on," Lisa said, taking Oliver's hand. "We need to get Ava."

They found Ava huddled in the shadows of the abandoned cabin, her slender form shaking with silent sobs. Her eyes, usually so full of fire, now mirrored the terror of the night's events.

"Lisa, Oliver," she whispered, her voice a thread of sound. "I was so scared. I thought I wouldn't see you again."

"Shh, it's over now. You're safe," Lisa assured her, pulling Ava into a tight embrace. Ava's body trembled against hers, and Lisa could feel her own heart pounding, not just from the exertion but from the fierce protectiveness that surged within her.

"Daniel's waiting for you at our place," Oliver said, his presence a solid reassurance in the darkness. "He's been asking for his mom."

Ava's eyes filled with tears, reflecting the moonlight. "Thank you," she murmured, clutching at Lisa as if anchoring herself to reality.

"Let's go home," Lisa said, a warm certainty filling her voice. She took Ava's hand in one of hers, Oliver's in the other, forming a chain of resolve and care. "I called the sheriff and told him to go to the cannery and what he'd find there. He'll take care of them."

: Chapter Eleven

Ava's phone buzzed on the kitchen counter, the screen lighting up with an ominous glow that sliced through the quaint warmth of Lisa and Oliver's home, where she had been staying for some weeks. She wiped her hands on a dish towel and then read the message that had popped up. Then, she grew pale. Seeing this, Lisa walked over to her.

"What's going on, Ava? What is it?"

She lifted the phone so Lisa could see what the text said:

"The past isn't buried. Neither are you… yet."

Ava broke into tears and ran out of the kitchen, crying. A chill skittered down Lisa's spine, erasing the comfort brought by the scent of freshly baked bread and the laughter of her children playing in the living room. Oliver was sanding down a piece of driftwood at the kitchen table and saw the color drain from her face.

"Lisa? What's wrong?" His voice was a rough caress, edged with concern.

She couldn't speak; the words stuck like thorns in her throat. Instead, she thrust the phone into his calloused hands, her eyes wide with fear. The message glared back at them, a silent threat that echoed the danger they thought they'd left behind.

"Ava just received this."

Oliver's jaw tightened, the charming smile that so often played on his lips replaced by a hard, determined line. "We need to move, and fast," he said, the timbre of his voice low and urgent. He grabbed his phone and called Sheriff Coleman. They spoke for what felt like an eternity to Lisa before he hung up.

Oliver sighed. "The sheriff and all his deputies are dealing with something on the other side of town. Since a crime hasn't been committed and it's just a threat, he can't rush off until they're done with what they're doing. By the time they make it here, it might be too late. I don't think we can risk that."

"Okay," Lisa said. "We know what we must do then."

"Daddy, look what I made!" Daniel bounded into the kitchen, brandishing a crayon drawing of a lopsided house with smoke billowing from its chimney.

Lisa knelt, her wavy hair brushing against Daniel's cheek as she pulled him close. "We're going to play a game, okay? A scavenger hunt."

"Can Mommy play too?" Daniel asked, his innocent question piercing her heart.

"Of course," she replied, mustering a smile for the

boy. She looked over to Oliver, who nodded, understanding the unspoken plan forming between them.

"Kids, listen up!" Oliver called out, using his "captain-on-deck" voice that never failed to command attention. "We're going on an adventure, just like the ones we read about in your books. We need to pack some things and stick together. Can I trust my brave crew to help?"

Eager nods and excited chatter filled the room as Lisa and Oliver swept into action. Oliver gathered the children, talking them through what they needed to do, while Lisa went to find Ava, who was in the backyard, her long dark hair lifting in the wind.

"Ava, we have to leave now," Lisa's voice was firm yet gentle, and the urgency was evident in her gaze.

Ava's eyes met Lisa's, a thousand unsaid words passing between them. Without hesitation, she scooped up Daniel, whispered something in his ear that made his eyes widen, and hurried inside.

The atmosphere was thick with worry and unanswered questions as they each grabbed essentials. Who were these people who kept coming after Ava? The sheriff had told them the pursuers left at the cannery all were wanted men for crimes committed somewhere else, so they were now in custody and would be prosecuted for those crimes and what they did to Oliver and Lisa. But these men could only have been messengers for whoever wanted to hurt Ava. So, where were these threats coming from? Why wouldn't they stop?

They worked silently and efficiently, the bonds of family and unspoken love driving them forward. Every

second counted, every heartbeat a drumroll of anticipation.

Lisa zipped shut the last of the heavy-duty backpacks,
her hands steady despite the turmoil brewing within.
The sharp tang of pine mingled with the musty scent
of leather that permeated their modest living room
was a reminder of Oliver's woodworking skills and the
countless hours he spent shaping wood into something
magical. Now, those same callused hands were wrapping blankets around supplies, protective and precise.

"Deep in the Alaskan wilderness, there's a place
not many know about," Oliver said, his voice hushed
as if sharing a sacred secret. It's an old cabin, well-
hidden and well-stocked. It belongs to my grandfather,
but he's an old man, he hasn't been there in many
years since it's very impassable terrain. We'll be safe
there."

Lisa watched as the children's eyes sparkled at the
mention of a hidden cabin. Their innocence was a
stark contrast to the reason for their hasty departure.
She nodded, drawing strength from Oliver's calm
demeanor. "Then that's where we'll go. It'll be like
those stories we tell by the fireplace. Only this time,
we're living it."

With each item secured in the trunk of their reli-
able four-wheel-drive—canned goods, bottled water,
matches, and first aid kits—a plan formulated in Lisa's
mind. Maps scattered across the kitchen table were

quickly studied, and routes memorized. She paused to add extra layers of clothing to the pile, her mind running through every possible scenario they might face.

"Mom, are we going camping?" Ethan's small voice trembled with a mixture of excitement and uncertainty.

"Something like that," Lisa replied, sweeping him into a hug that conveyed all the reassurance she could muster. "A special kind of camping where we look out for each other and stay close, like wolves in a pack."

As Oliver locked the doors and windows, the silence between them spoke volumes. Lisa threw a last glance over her shoulder at the cozy home that had been their refuge, praying that they would be back soon. Her heart ached, but the maternal instinct to safeguard her kin spurred her on.

"Let's go, my loves," she called, ushering the children toward the truck where Ava waited, Daniel clutched tightly in her arms. Their faces were set, a mirror of Lisa's determination.

They climbed into the vehicle, the engine coming to life with a comforting purr. Oliver maneuvered them onto the road, his eyes scanning the rearview mirror more often than usual. The path ahead wound into dense forests and rugged terrain, where the promise of solitude beckoned.

The road unspooled under the car like a gray ribbon, flanked by towering pines that whispered secrets of the deep Alaskan wilderness. Oliver's hands gripped the steering wheel with quiet resolve as he navigated each bend and rise in the landscape. The children's soft breathing was intermittent with the sound of tires crunching gravel—a lullaby of motion and hope.

"Mom, are we almost there?" Abigail's voice cut through the monotony, tinged with a mix of excitement and weariness.

"Soon, sweetheart," Lisa replied, turning around and offering a reassuring smile.

Her eyes flicked back to the road, then to the mirror again—this time lingering longer than before. A knot tightened in her stomach as she caught sight of a vehicle that hadn't been behind them when they'd started their journey. Its presence was an anomaly on this seldom-used back route.

"Oliver," she said, her voice steady despite the chill crawling up her spine, "we have company."

He straightened in his seat, the playful glint in his blue eyes replaced by steely alertness. He looked in the mirror, observing the car that seemed to eat up the distance between them with hungry determination.

"Any idea who it might be?" she asked, her heart pounding frantically against her ribs.

"None," Oliver murmured, the lines of his face hardening. "But we're not taking any chances."

Lisa's mind raced. She thought of the message on Ava's phone, the words that had disrupted their peace, and felt the protective lioness within her awaken.

"I'll keep an eye on them," she instructed, her tone leaving no room for argument. She turned her back to watch the pursuing vehicle. "You focus on the driving."

"You got it," Oliver assured her, his hand sliding down next to his seat, where discreetly placed—where the children couldn't see—he clutched his gun.

Lisa focused on the car behind them. The persistent presence of the vehicle in the mirror gnawed at her sense of safety. She remembered Oliver showing her the hidden trails and shortcuts, paths not marked on any map and known only to those who called this untamed land home.

"Oliver," whispered Lisa, her voice taut with urgency, "it's getting closer."

He nodded, feeling the weight of their family's lives balanced delicately in his hands. In the driver's seat, he was more than a father, a lover, a business partner; he was the guardian of their collective future, steering them through uncertainty toward the promise of refuge.

"Everything will be okay," he said, more to himself than to Lisa or the children. And as the suspicious car edged nearer, he pressed his foot gently onto the accelerator, his resolve as unyielding as the wilderness surrounding them.

Oliver's grip on the wheel tightened, his knuckles whitening as the engine roared in protest. The rearview mirror framed the ominous approach of their pursuer, a darkened silhouette that seemed to grow larger with each passing second. Lisa's hand rested on his shoulder—a silent plea for reassurance— as the children's hushed whispers filled the backseat. Ava sat completely still, only turning around now and then to see if the car was still there, her face pale, her eyes big with anxiety.

"We've got this," Lisa murmured.

Gritting his teeth, Oliver pushed the pedal further, coaxing every ounce of power from their weary vehicle. It lurched forward, straining against the limit of its capabilities. In the passenger seat, Lisa's gaze flitted between the chasing vehicle and the path ahead, her body tensed for action.

"Left, up here, there's an old logging trail," Oliver said, pointing to a barely visible break in the dense foliage.

Without hesitation, he swung the car onto the narrow path, branches scraping against metal like fingernails on a chalkboard. The pursuers, unprepared for the sudden detour, lagged behind, their headlights faltering amidst the thick underbrush.

"Good call," Lisa praised quietly, her breaths measured and controlled despite the adrenaline coursing through her veins.

Oliver merely nodded, his eyes scanning the rearview mirror for any sign of the encroaching threat.

The car bounced over roots and rocks, a testament to Oliver's intimate knowledge of this hidden artery through the wild heart of Alaska. He was one with the landscape, attuned to its secrets and safe havens.

A sharp turn loomed ahead, and he navigated it with precision, the barest slip of the tires on the dirt track betraying the haste of their flight. The children let out a collective gasp, a mix of excitement and anxiety, as they clung to each other, their world reduced to the confines of the car and the sound of their mother's steady heartbeat.

"Almost there, just a bit more," Lisa whispered, though whether it was a promise or a prayer, she couldn't tell. Oliver reached across to squeeze her hand, a fleeting connection charged with unspoken emotions.

"Almost there."

The engine roared as Oliver pushed the pedal, urging every ounce of power from their weary vehicle. Lisa glanced in the rearview mirror, her breath catching as headlights pierced the twilight behind them. They had been so close, the silence almost convincing her they were alone, but now the threat loomed again, a monstrous shadow creeping ever closer.

"Oliver," she hissed, her voice barely above a whisper, "they're back."

He swiveled in his seat, his eyes scanning the encroaching darkness. "Damn it," he muttered, the lines on his forehead deepening. "We can't let them catch us."

The children's murmurs of fear bled into the tense air, but Oliver's resolve hardened like ice. His fingers gripped the wheel until his knuckles whitened again.

"Oliver, look out!" Lisa's shout snapped him back into focus as the enemy car surged forward.

Without a second thought, he wrenched the wheel to the right, veering off the road. The world outside became a blur as the car plunged into the dense embrace of the forest. Branches clawed at the windows, leaves fluttered in violent waves, and the earth beneath them turned treacherous with undergrowth.

"Keep your heads down!" Lisa commanded, her protective instincts in full throttle as Oliver navigated around ancient trunks and over uneven terrain.

The vehicle jolted and skidded, a wild dance between control and chaos. Lisa's hands hovered over the dashboard, ready to brace for impact, yet she never uttered a word of doubt. Her silent trust in Oliver was palpable.

"Are we going to be okay, Mom?" a small voice piped up from the back, quivering with the weight of the unknown.

"Yes," Lisa replied, her fear smothered by the fierce determination that resonated with her words. "I promise you."

The pursuing lights faltered, confused by the thicket that now shielded them from sight. Oliver maneuvered the car behind a cluster of dense foliage, cutting the engine and plunging them into an eerie stillness. Each breath seemed too loud, each heartbeat a drumroll to an uncertain finale.

"Stay quiet," Oliver whispered as they waited, the suspense wrapping around them like a thick fog. The only sound was the distant thrum of the other vehicle, its driver searching for a trail that had vanished like smoke.

Together, they sat in the hushed sanctuary of the forest, their bodies pressed close, a single unit woven with threads of hope and unyielding love. In the pitch-black woods, hidden from the hunters, Lisa held onto the warmth of Oliver's hand, their entwined fingers a testament to a bond that no chase could unravel. And soon, the pursuing car gave up, then took off, disappearing into the darkness. Lisa breathed in relief. Oliver twisted the key in the ignition, then let out a breath that sounded like a gasp.

"What's going on?" Lisa asked.

"The truck won't start." Oliver turned the key, and it clicked eerily but didn't turn on. Seeing this, Lisa felt panic welling up in her chest. "Well, what do we do?"

"My grandfather's cabin isn't far from here," he said. "We can walk."

Lisa's breaths came in sharp gasps, the cold air biting at her lungs as she led the way through the underbrush. Each step was careful and calculated to avoid snapping twigs or rustling leaves too loudly. Oliver was right behind her, carrying Daniel on his back, his strides silent despite the child's weight. Ava clutched the hands of Lisa's children, her knuckles white with the effort to keep them close and quiet. Luckily, Julia was sound asleep in the carrier strapped onto Lisa's chest.

The forest seemed to close in around them, the darkness engulfing them. Lisa's hair was plastered to her forehead, and her eyes were scanning for signs of movement or the glint of headlights. She could feel Oliver's presence like a steady light, his unwavering determination a comfort amidst the chaos.

"Daddy, where are we going?" The whisper from Daniel was barely audible, but to Lisa, it rang out like a siren call.

"Shh," she soothed, turning to press a finger against her lips. "We're playing a game, remember? We need to be as quiet as mice."

A nod, big eyes wide with fear and trust, and they continued onward.

"It's getting too dark to see," Oliver said.

Lisa could sense the desperation in his voice.

"What do you mean?" she asked.

"I can't seem to find the way to the cabin."

"What does that mean? We need to get to it," she whispered.

After what felt like an eternity but was likely only minutes, Lisa spotted a rocky outcrop ahead. With a tug on Oliver's hand, she veered toward it, the outline of a hidden cave coming into view.

"This will do," she whispered.

Heart pounding, she ushered everyone inside, the darkness enveloping them like a protective shroud.

They huddled together, the cave's damp walls offering scant comfort against the chill. Oliver set Daniel down, affectionately ruffling the boy's messy dark hair, trying to inject a sense of normalcy into the fraught situation.

"Good hiding spot," he murmured, his voice a low rumble in the compact space.

Lisa pulled her children closer, wrapping them in an embrace that was both a shield and a reassurance. Ava sat beside them, her eyes reflecting the flicker of fear and resolve that Lisa knew mirrored her own.

Oliver used his phone's light so they could see.

Lisa met his gaze, her warm smile a silent promise amidst the uncertainty. They were a team, bound by something stronger than fear—love and a shared will to survive. They were momentarily untouchable in this hidden crevice of the world, their hearts beating a collective rhythm of hope and courage.

They sat like that until just after midnight, when they suddenly heard voices coming from outside the cave.

The echo of their ragged breaths filled the cave as Lisa's mind whirred with strategic precision. The voices were coming closer, the sound bouncing against the tree trunks, yet they were still distant.

"We need a distraction," she whispered, her voice

steady despite the tremor of fear that quivered through her limbs. Her eyes met Oliver's, finding an unspoken agreement there.

"Flares," Oliver responded, nodding at the pack he'd managed to grab before they fled. He pulled two bright red cylinders out, a fisherman's survival tool. "It could work. It'll draw their eyes—and hopefully them —long enough for you all to get a head start."

Lisa's heart clenched at the thought of separation, but she knew it was their best shot. She nodded, her lips pressed into a thin line of resolve.

"Take the west route toward the creek," he instructed Ava, who listened intently. "Follow it down-stream until you see the three pines shaped like a 'W.' That's where we'll meet. Use my phone as a flashlight."

Oliver knelt before their children, his eyes soft but fierce. "Listen to Ava, okay? Mom and I have to make sure those bad guys don't follow you." His words were simple, yet they carried the weight of promises and the strength of his will.

Ava clasped Lisa's hand briefly, her eyes offering silent support, before turning to gather Daniel in her arms. The child's innocent gaze flitted between the adults, sensing the gravity of farewell without under-standing its full context.

"Be brave, my loves," Lisa murmured, pressing a kiss to each of her children's foreheads, her hair falling like a curtain around their huddle. Oliver's arm encir-cled them all for one fleeting moment—a bastion in a stormy sea.

"Remember, Dad loves you more than all the stars in the sky," Oliver said, his voice catching on the swell of emotions. His hands were gentle as they brushed away the worry lines from their young faces.

"I will be right there," Lisa added, her smile wavering like a candle flame in the wind. She tucked the memory of their embrace deep within her heart, fuel for the trials ahead.

With great care, they untangled themselves from the embrace and stood, facing the mouth of the cave. Lisa's hand found Oliver's, their fingers locking together in silent unity. They both peered into the thickening darkness outside, where the unknown loomed.

"Go now, quickly and quietly," Lisa urged, her voice a soft command. As Ava ushered the children into the shadows of the trees, Lisa released Oliver's hand, feeling the lingering warmth like a promise.

"See you soon," she said, forcing confidence into her tone.

Lisa watched them disappear into the forest, her chest tight with love and fear. Then, turning back to Oliver, she felt the adrenaline surge.

"Ready?" Oliver asked, his gaze locked onto hers.

"Ready," Lisa answered. Together, they stepped forward, ready to face whatever came next with the courage of those who fight not just for survival but for love.

Then, they set off the signals. Red light blasted up in the sky, and they could hear yelling as the pursuers took up the chase.

Leaves crunched underfoot as Lisa and Oliver plunged deeper into the wilderness, an expanse of shadows and whispers. Their breaths frosted the air, mingling with the night's mist that curled around them like wraiths. They moved with purpose, each step propelling them further from their children, each stride a silent declaration of war against the unseen enemy.

"Head to the ridge," Oliver murmured, his voice barely louder than the rustle of the underbrush.

Lisa could feel the thrum of the earth beneath her boots, the heartbeat of the wild that had become their temporary ally.

Oliver's hand brushed hers, an anchor in the surge of uncertainty. "We can lose them there," he added, his eyes scanning the dense thicket for signs of pursuit.

They reached a clearing, moonlight piercing the canopy in silver shafts, casting ghostly patterns on the forest floor. Lisa's heart raced as she glanced back, half-expecting to see the shadow of their pursuers looming over them. But there was only the forest—silent, watchful, and vast.

"Keep moving," Oliver urged, his voice laced with the strain of their flight.

With the precision of a woodworker carving his path, Oliver led them along a barely discernible trail marked only by the subtle signs he had come to recognize. Every so often, he would pause, tilting his head to catch the faintest sound, the distant snap of a twig, or the soft tread of danger. Lisa stayed close, her senses heightened to every nuance of the night.

A sudden crack echoed through the trees, sharp and ominous, fracturing the stillness. Lisa's pulse spiked, and she tightened her grip on the makeshift weapon clutched in her hand—a sturdy branch she'd picked up along the way, its weight reassuring against her palm.

"Here," Oliver said, pointing to a cluster of rocks draped in moss. They crouched behind it, their bodies taut with anticipation, ready to spring. Oliver's dark hair fell across his forehead, a stark contrast against the paleness of his face. His eyes met Lisa's in the moonlight, an unspoken message passing between them—they were in this together, whatever the end might be.

"Remember the plan," Lisa whispered, her thoughts drifting to the kids, Ava, and the life they were fighting to reclaim. Her love for them burned fierce and bright, fueling her resolve. "If we split up—"

"Shh." Oliver's hand on her arm stilled her words. Movement flickered at the edge of her vision, a shadow detaching itself from the darkness.

"Go!" It was a shout and a whisper all at once, and they broke cover, sprinting away from the rocks, drawing the danger with them.

Their lungs screamed, muscles burning as they pushed their bodies beyond limits, every footfall a defiance of fear. The ground blurred beneath them, the forest a maze of adrenaline and will.

"Lisa!" Oliver's voice cut through the clamor of their escape. She turned just in time to see him stumble, a root catching his ankle. She was at his side in an instant, pulling him to his feet, their partnership unyielding even as chaos unfurled around them.

"Keep going!" he urged, the pain etched onto his face overshadowed by the determination in his eyes.

Together, they ran, their love a silent chant in the rhythm of their steps, their sacrifice a testament to the depth of their bond. They charged into the heart of peril, unwavering and brave for their family and each other.

They took a turn minutes later, and Oliver believed it seemed familiar. "We're on track for the cabin again," he said. "I used to play here as a child."

Oliver sighed with relief as he saw the cabin once they ran through a row of trees. This could provide them with shelter. For now.

Chapter Twelve

The rugged door of the cabin slammed shut with a resounding thud, its aged wood groaning under the weight of desperation. Oliver's chest heaved as he slid the deadbolt into place, his broad shoulders rising and falling in tandem with Lisa's frantic breaths. Shadows enveloped them. The only light was the moonlight seeping through the cracks in the timbered walls. The air was electric with anxiety, their shared pulse thundering loud enough to drown out the encroaching footsteps from outside.

"Oliver," Lisa whispered, her voice barely audible over the cacophony of their heartbeats. She clutched at his flannel shirt, seeking solace in the solid warmth of his presence. Her eyes darted around the dimly lit interior, looking for any sign of reassurance in this maelstrom of fear.

"Shh, it's going to be okay," he mouthed back, though his uncertainty gnawed at him. The familiar scent of sawdust clinging to his skin reminded him of his workshop, a sanctuary that now felt worlds away.

Their bodies pressed against the rough logs, and the couple crouched low beneath a dust-covered window. Outside, the rustling of leaves and snapping twigs intensified, signaling their pursuers' unwavering proximity. Oliver's hand moved to the gun, its weight a grim comfort. His fingers traced the handle, each movement a silent testament to his determination to protect their sanctuary, their life together.

As if on cue, gunshots shattered the silence, bullets piercing the night and embedding themselves into the cabin's exterior. Splinters flew like deadly confetti, a stark reminder of how fragile their shelter was.

"Down!" Oliver commanded, pulling Lisa closer to the ground and shielding her with his body. His heart throbbed in his ears, a relentless drum pushing him past the edge of fear into action. He rose just enough to peek through the window, the gun now cradled in his trembling hands.

Lisa's breath hitched, her chest tightening with every shot Oliver fired into the dark abyss beyond their refuge. Each blast was a defiant cry, an echo of the small-town resilience that had bound them to this place and each other.

The moonlight cast a pale glow over the chamber, illuminating Oliver's determined face. It was a countenance carved from the same wood he lovingly shaped by day, now hardened by the resolve to keep the danger at bay. His jaw clenched with each recoil, and his normally kind eyes narrowed into steely slits of focus.

A shiver of terror raced down Lisa's spine, her mind reeling with images of her children—Ethan's wide, frightened eyes, Abigail's trembling hands, Julia's silent cries. The thought of them lost and alone in the woods was almost too much to bear. But then she clung to the lifeline of hope: Ava had taken them to safety. She would have led them away from danger by now, toward the shadowy embrace of the forest where threats were hidden but so was refuge.

"Oliver," she whispered, her voice barely carrying over the pounding in her chest, "the kids...."

He didn't need to look at her to understand; their connection ran deeper than words. They shared a glance, and in his nod, she found the unspoken promise that they would do everything to return to their children.

The cabin walls creaked ominously, and the splintering sound of wood pierced the night air. Someone was at the door, pulling the doorknob. Hearing this, Lisa gasped. Then, the person kicked the door hard, and it splintered. An intruder was using brute force, trying to break through their sanctuary's defenses. Oliver's stance shifted, the gun becoming an extension of his will to protect. His fingers wrapped around the weapon with a craftsman's familiarity, but now it wasn't the curve of a chair or the smooth finish of a table he sought—it was the preservation of life.

"Stay behind me," he instructed, his voice low and steady despite the adrenaline coursing through his veins.

Lisa pressed herself against the wall, her heart aching with a cocktail of fear and gratitude. She knew without a doubt that Oliver would lay down his life for her and their family. But was she willing to lose him? Absolutely not. He moved with quiet intensity, inching closer to the door, ready to unleash a storm upon whoever dared to threaten their last bastion of safety.

The door buckled under another heavy blow, splinters flying like desperate escapes from the inevitable invasion. A gun came into sight; it was held by the intruder and pointed at them. And then, as if in slow motion, Oliver raised his gun. The small room seemed to contract, focusing all energy on the space between the man and the door that was about to give way.

"Come on," he muttered under his breath, not to Lisa but to himself, to the universe, to the very fabric of fate that held their lives in its unpredictable grip.

The remains of the door burst open with a violent crash, and Oliver fired—the shot deafening, echoing through the cabin and into the night.

&

The gunshot's echo faded, replaced by a haunting silence that wrapped around Oliver like a suffocating shroud. He stood motionless, the gun's weight in his hands now mirroring the heaviness in his soul as he stared at the body on the floor in front of him. Each breath he drew seemed to quiver with the tremors of their predicament, and for an instant, the world outside the splintered door ceased to exist.

Oliver's eyes, dark pools reflecting the chaos he had just unleashed, searched the room's shadows—a room that had transformed from sanctuary to battlefield in mere heartbeats. His chest rose and fell in rapid succession, each inhale sharp with the sting of gunpowder and fear, each exhale a silent plea for safety, for resolve, for the children who were his entire world.

"Oliver," Lisa's voice pierced the fog of his paralysis, her tone threaded with urgency and the ironclad will to survive that he had come to know—no, to revere—in her. Her hand, warm and trembling, found his, a lifeline amidst the storm of uncertainty that threatened to claim them both.

"Oliver, we have to go. Now." Her words were a clarion call, snapping him back to the grim reality they faced.

He blinked, his gaze locking onto hers. Those hazel eyes held within them the fires of determination and the softness of love—all that was worth fighting for. And in that moment, it wasn't the practiced calm of a woodworker or the stoic strength of a fisherman he summoned; it was the raw, unyielding spirit of a man driven by love and the primal instinct to protect his family.

"Right," he muttered, the single syllable carrying the weight of his renewed resolve. The gun still in one hand, he allowed her to lead him, her grip on his hand firm and sure, toward the back door—a promising escape from the closing jaws of danger, while the sound of approaching footsteps fueled their fear.

Their flight was a dance of shadows, a silent choreography of desperate hope as they slipped out into the cool embrace of the night air. Lisa steered them away from the looming threat, her maternal ferocity a force unto itself. Oliver's heart raced, syncing with hers in a rhythm of shared purpose: to live, love, and fight another day for their family's tomorrow.

The forest swallowed them, its towering trees casting long fingers of shadow that crisscrossed their path. Oliver and Lisa's breaths came in gasps, white puffs spiraling into the blackened air as they plunged deeper into the woods. Overhead, the moon carved a silver swath through the tangle of branches, offering scant pools of light by which to navigate the perilous terrain. Each step was a gamble, each rustle a potential herald of danger lurking just beyond the next tree.

Lisa's shoulder-length hair whipped behind her like a battle standard, her senses heightened to every snap of twigs beneath their feet. The cool night air did nothing to soothe the burning in her lungs, but she pushed on, her hand a lifeline entwined with Oliver's, anchoring him to the urgency of their flight.

Suddenly, the sharp trill of her phone cleaved through the silence, and Lisa's heart lurched. She stumbled, nearly losing her footing on the uneven ground, but Oliver's grip steadied her. Fumbling with the device, her eyes widened as she registered the name illuminated on the screen—Oliver's phone.

"Hello?" Her voice was a whisper thrumming with hope and fear.

"Mom?" The single word, so fraught with emotion, had her heart constricting painfully. It wasn't Ava, yet hearing Ethan's voice was both a balm and a torment, a reminder of what was at stake.

"Where are you? Are you safe?" Lisa pressed the phone hard to her ear, straining to hear over the pounding of her own blood.

"I think so, but…" Ethan replied, his voice small against the backdrop of the wild. He went quiet.

"Ethan?" Lisa's voice was barely above a whisper, an undercurrent of fear lacing her words as she clutched Oliver's arm.

"Mom!" Ethan's voice cracked over the line, his breaths coming in frantic gasps that tugged at Lisa's soul. "Ava and Daniel—they took them."

The world seemed to tilt on its axis, the moonlight suddenly too harsh, the shadows too deep. Lisa's knees weakened, but Oliver's grip was steady, unwavering.

"Who, Ethan? Who took them?" Her voice rose in panic, each word sharp with terror.

"I—I don't know," he sobbed, the sound of his

cries twisting like a knife in her chest. "We were hiding, and they just… grabbed them and ran."

Lisa's mind reeled, images of her children—terrified and alone—flashing before her eyes. "And Julia? Is she—"

"She's with me," Ethan rushed to assure her, a small solace amidst the chaos threatening to consume her. "So is Abigail."

"Where are you now?" she asked, struggling to keep her voice steady for her son's sake.

"At the creek," he sniffled, his voice a light in the oppressive darkness. "We're at the creek, Mom."

"Stay hidden, do you hear me? We'll be there as soon as we can." The maternal command in her tone was underscored by a raw determination.

Ethan's next breath hitched, a silent understanding passing between mother and son. "Okay, Mom. Hurry."

The call ended, leaving a void filled only by the ragged sound of their breathing and the distant murmur of the creek. Lisa locked eyes with Oliver, his blue gaze reflecting the tumultuous swirl of emotions within her—fear, love, and an unyielding resolve.

They turned together, moving with a newfound urgency. Every rustle of leaves was a potential threat, and every snapped twig a signal to move faster. The air around them grew thick with suspense, the woods alive with unseen dangers.

❧

The moon hung low, a pale guardian in the sky as Lisa and Oliver darted between the trees, their breaths misting in the chilled air. The forest was a labyrinth of shadows, each holding the possibility of danger, but Lisa's thoughts were consumed by the image of her children hiding by the creek. Her gut twisted at the thought of what might happen if their pursuers discovered Ethan, Abigail, and Julia, every dark scenario clawing at her resolve.

"Stay hidden; do you hear me? We'll be there as soon as we can," she had told Ethan, her voice a tremulous blend of command and comfort. She clung to the hope that her words would fortify her son's courage, praying they would remain unseen in the brush.

"Lisa, this way." Oliver's hand found hers, pulling her through a particularly dense patch of under-growth. Branches snagged at her hair and clothes, but the thorns of worry pricking at her heart were sharper still. She could not—would not—let fear cripple her when her children needed her most.

"Oliver, if they..." Her voice trailed off, the unspoken fears too harrowing to articulate. But she didn't need to finish the sentence; Oliver's squeeze on her hand said everything. They would face whatever came together.

"Lisa, look at me." Oliver halted, urgency lacing his tone. She stilled, meeting his gaze, finding an echo of her own determination mirrored there. "We'll make it to them. We've got to keep moving."

Reassured by his steadfast presence, Lisa nodded,

swallowing back the panic that threatened to choke her.

"Ethan, Abigail, Julia… I have to get to them," she whispered more to herself than to Oliver, channeling her love into raw momentum. With renewed fervor, she pushed forward, leading them deeper into the heart of the woods.

Every snapped twig beneath their feet felt like a thunderclap in the silence, every rustle a potential alarm. Yet, with each step, Lisa's maternal instinct outshone her trepidation, propelling her onward. The forest's darkness couldn't compare to the light of her love, a flame that refused to be extinguished by fear.

"Stay put, Ethan," she breathed into the night, a silent vow to safeguard the fragile innocence waiting for them. It was a race against time, a mother's pledge against the shadows. And Lisa was not one to break her word.

"Mommy is coming for you."

Branches whipped against Lisa's face as she and Oliver tore through the underbrush, their breaths heavy in the cold night air. The moon hung like a silver medallion in the sky, casting a deceptive calm over the dark woods that belied the peril they were in. They knew the creek lay ahead—Ethan's whispered plea echoed in Lisa's ears, urging them on.

Her legs burned with the effort, muscles protesting each desperate stride, yet she couldn't afford to slow down. The thought of her children huddled together by the water's edge, vulnerable and scared, was unbearable. Every second mattered now; every heartbeat was a drumbeat spurring them onward.

Oliver's hand tightened around hers, an unspoken vow that he would never let go. His resolve was her lifeline, the steadfast determination in his eyes an anchor amidst the chaos. Together, they were a force unto themselves—a whirlwind of courage spun from the deepest wells of parental love and tenacity.

"Almost there!" Oliver's voice cut through the silence, slicing through the tension.

Lisa's heart hammered against her ribs, its rhythm syncing with the forest's thrumming pulse. Adrenaline surged through her veins, lending her limbs a strength she didn't know she possessed. They skirted a thicket and dodged a gnarled tree root, and the sound of rushing water grew louder, promising a nearness to the children that kept panic at bay.

There was a rustle to their left—were they still being followed? The threat of their pursuers loomed over them, a sinister shadow that could pounce at any moment. But Lisa pushed the fear aside, focusing only on the path ahead. She had to be strong—for Oliver, for herself, and most importantly, for their children.

The creek's melody resonated through the trees, its song growing clearer with every lung-busting sprint. Lisa's thoughts whirled, grappling with the possibility of what they'd find upon arrival. Would they make it in time?

"Lisa, look!" Oliver pointed ahead, where the tree

line broke to reveal the silvery thread of the creek glistening in the moonlight.

With a final burst of energy, they broke free from the forest's grasp, stumbling toward the water's edge. Their eyes scanned the darkness for any sign of life, any hint of their beloved children.

And then they saw them.

Chapter Thirteen

Oliver's arms closed around Lisa in a fierce, protective embrace the moment they spotted the children across the babbling creek, and they ran to them.

"Mom! Ollie!"

They all hugged, and Lisa closed her eyes briefly, enjoying the moment while kissing her baby's head, who was cooing delightfully while dangling from her brother's chest. Relief flooded through Lisa's veins, mingling with an undercurrent of tension that refused to ebb away entirely. The absence of their pursuers hung in the air like an unanswered question, but for now, the family was reunited, and that was what mattered.

"Are they gone?" Lisa whispered, her voice barely audible over the rush of the water.

"For now," Oliver replied, his gaze scanning the dense foliage that bordered the creek, the stoic set of his jaw betraying his readiness to spring into action should danger resurface. "My guess is that now that they have Ava and Daniel, they have what they came for. They'll leave us alone."

"But that's awful," Lisa said.

"I know."

With tentative steps, they began to navigate through the forest, the oppressive grip of night gradually loosening as dawn's early light filtered through the towering canopy. A symphony of awakening birdsong accompanied their cautious progress, the flutelike calls weaving through the crisp morning air. Shafts of sunlight pierced the thicket, casting dappled patterns on the dew-kissed ferns that unfurled at their feet.

Lisa couldn't help but marvel at the serene beauty that enveloped them, the natural splendor of the woods offering a stark contrast to the fear that had driven them into its depths. She watched as the children's faces, previously etched with anxiety, softened in the growing daylight, the golden rays painting their features with a warmth that seemed to breathe life back into their weary spirits.

Oliver, too, appeared less like the hardened protector he'd become under the cloak of darkness and more the loving father and husband Lisa knew him to be. His careful steps were measured and deliberate, ensuring each child stayed close, his hands occasionally reaching out to brush a reassuring caress along Julia's sparse hair or steady Ethan's shoulder.

As the forest around them awoke to the new day, hope began to stir within Lisa's chest—a fragile bloom amidst the thorns of uncertainty. They were not out of danger yet, not by a long shot, but in this tranquil haven of nature, it was possible to believe, if only for a moment, that everything might just be okay.

Lisa's fingers clenched Oliver's as they wove through the underbrush, each step carrying them further from danger and closer to an uncertain future. The forest was a bastion of peace, yet her heart could find no rest, thrumming with concern for those not among their number.

"Oliver," she whispered, her voice barely audible above the rustle of leaves, "we need to talk about Ava and Daniel."

He glanced over, his brow furrowed with the same worry that gnawed at her insides.

"I know," he said, his voice heavy. "We will find a way to get them to safety."

The memory of Ava's fearful eyes haunted Lisa. Once, she had been consumed by jealousy toward the woman who had almost claimed Oliver's heart, but now, thinking of Ava being out there with little Daniel, possibly cold and scared, in the hands of people who wanted to hurt them, twisted Lisa's gut with compassion.

"Can we tell the sheriff what happened?" Lisa's gaze searched his face for a certainty she couldn't muster herself. Ava had told them not to tell the sheriff about her, as she, too, was wanted and would be arrested. Whatever she had been involved in had been criminal, but she assured them she only did it out of need—that she had no choice. So, Lisa and Oliver had agreed not to involve the sheriff any further. They hadn't told him what was really going on. They realized now that was a mistake. They should have talked to him from the beginning, told him everything, and asked for protection instead of running into the wilderness, thinking they could outsmart them.

"We will have to take that risk," Oliver replied, squeezing her hand. "For their sake. This is their lives we're talking about. We don't know what these people want with them."

Ethan, ever perceptive, fell into step beside them. His young green eyes had seen too much, yet they held a resilience that stirred pride in Lisa's chest.

"Mom, Ollie," Ethan began, his tone earnest, "Ava and Daniel… are they going to be okay? We can't just leave them, can we?"

Lisa exchanged a look with Oliver, both touched and heartbroken at the young boy's concern. "We're going to do everything we can, sweetheart," she assured him, her throat tight. "They're family."

"Like you always say, Mom—family sticks together." Ethan nodded, his expression set with a determination that echoed theirs.

"Exactly, Ethan," Oliver said, ruffling his hair. "And we'll stick together through all of this."

Their path continued, the dappled light guiding them steadily onward, each step a silent promise to the ones left behind: They would find Ava and Daniel and bring them home.

Abigail's small hand slipped from Lisa's grasp, her knees buckling like frail branches under the weight of fatigue.

"Mommy," she whimpered, the word barely escaping her lips before she crumpled onto the forest floor, her long brown hair spilling over the leaves like autumn's blanket.

"Abby!" Lisa's heart constricted as she dropped to her daughter's side, sweeping the girl into her arms. The physical strain etched lines of worry across her face, mirrored by Oliver as he moved closer, his strong hands gently lifting Abigail.

"We've got you, darling," Oliver said, his voice a soothing balm, even as his muscles protested silently under the additional burden. They walked side by side as he carried Abigail, her breaths shallow against the chirping backdrop of the woods, which seemed oblivious to the gravity of their plight.

Each step felt heavier than the last, the forest's beauty now a stark contrast to the weight of uncertainty bearing down on them. Lisa glanced at Ethan, his youthful features set in grim determination, carrying his baby sister—their children, their world.

"Oliver," Lisa murmured, her voice threadbare, "I just want to go home."

"Home," Oliver echoed as though the word itself were sanctuary. He nodded, the decision settling within him. "Yes, we'll go home." His eyes met hers, a silent pact forged between them. It had been a mistake to come out here.

But as the trees began to thin, revealing the first glimpses of morning light, the question loomed unspoken in the crisp air: Where were Ava and Daniel now? And how would they keep the promise made to Ethan—never to leave family behind?

The tangle of branches broke away, and there it was —the main road, a gray ribbon unfurling through the lush greenery. Oliver's shoulders sagged with relief as he stepped out of the forest's embrace. Ethan trudged alongside them, his gaze fixed on the familiar path that heralded safety.

"Look," Ethan breathed out, pointing. The sight of the asphalt meant cars, people, and the comforting buzz of civilization.

"Thank God," Lisa whispered, her voice a blend of awe and exhaustion. She took Abigail in her arms to relieve Oliver for a little, feeling her daughter's small body lean into her, seeking comfort.

Oliver scanned the road, his protective instincts on high alert. It was quiet, too quiet for his liking, until the sound of an engine hummed in the distance. His hand instinctively rose, fingers stretched wide.

"Come on," he urged, striding toward the edge of the road where gravel met the verge of the wilderness they had just escaped.

"Please, stop!" Lisa called out, her voice laced with an urgency that made Ethan echo her plea.

"Stop, please!" he shouted, his young voice cracking.

The truck, an old blue pickup, rumbled closer, its engine's growl growing louder with each heartbeat. For a moment, it seemed as though it would pass them by, but then brake lights flashed red, and with a sigh like a tired beast settling down to rest, it rolled to a stop.

"Need help?" the driver—a man with a weathered face and kind eyes—hollered through the open window.

"Could you take us to town?" Oliver asked, his tone rough with gratitude. "Our kids are exhausted, and we've been through a lot."

"Of course, hop on."

Lisa managed a weary smile, climbing into the bed of the truck with Ethan's assistance, Abigail still nestled in her arms. Ethan's eyes were wide with the responsibility he felt for his family, and he adjusted Julia in her carrier, then kissed her forehead, making sure she was settled safely.

"Thank you," Lisa said again, sharing a look with Oliver that conveyed words they didn't need to speak. Their family was safe, for now—but their journey was far from over.

As the old blue pickup rattled down the road, they all sat close together in the back, the wind pulling at their tired faces. Oliver wrapped his arm tighter around Lisa, her head resting against his shoulder. The truck's steady hum was a comforting contrast to the chaos they'd fled. He could feel her body tense with unspoken thoughts, the same ones that were racing through his mind.

"Once we get home," Oliver murmured, his voice barely audible over the engine's roar, "we'll figure out our next move together."

Lisa lifted her gaze to meet his, and he saw the reflection of his determination in her eyes. "We'll find them," she said, the words a promise, "Ava and Daniel… We have to."

The driver glanced at them through the rearview mirror, sensing the gravity of their situation. As they neared the town, buildings emerging like specters from the fog of dawn, the couple shared a moment of quiet resolve. They knew the risks ahead, the secrets that lurked in the shadows of their small town, waiting to be brought into the light.

The familiar storefronts were now passing by in a blur, each one a reminder of the life they fought so hard to build. But beneath the heartwarming sight of their community, there hid an undercurrent of danger, a threat that had already touched their lives more than they cared to admit.

The truck slowed as it approached the edge of town, and the driver turned to them once more.

"Where to?" he asked, shouting out of the window, his voice kind but laced with curiosity.

"Main Street," Oliver instructed, pointing toward their café. "Drop us off there."

"Got it." The driver nodded and turned back to the road.

As they disembarked onto the familiar pavement, they profusely thanked the driver, who tipped his hat and drove away, leaving them in the slowly brightening day. They watched the truck disappear around a corner, feeling the weight of isolation settle upon them once again.

Oliver took a deep breath, the cool morning air filling his lungs with a mix of dread and anticipation. "We have to be smart about this, Lisa. We don't know who we can trust."

"Except each other," she replied firmly, gripping his hand. "We'll start with the places Ava might have been taken. This is a small area. Think, Oliver. Think where they could be kept without anyone knowing."

"Let's get the kids settled first. Then we plan."

They walked toward their cafe; their haven turned into a makeshift command center. Behind the warmth and comfort of their everyday life, the gears of their minds turned, plotting a course through the unknown.

"Oliver," Lisa whispered, her voice tight with urgency as they reached the door, "what if we're already too late?"

He met her gaze, allowing no room for fear. "We're not," he said. "We can't be."

Chapter Fourteen

L isa's fingers flew across the keyboard, a flurry of urgency as she scoured the internet for schematics of the abandoned mill on the outskirts of town. They had narrowed it down, and this had to be it, they agreed. It was the only place it could be if they kept them around here. It was worth a shot. The dilapidated structure, shrouded in local folklore and an air of menace, was where they believed Daniel and Ava were being held captive. They had even been staking the place out and seen suspicious-looking types come and go. Types that very much resembled the men who had chased them through the woods.

"Here," she breathed out, pointing at the monitor. "I found an old floor plan. It'll help us navigate once we're inside."

Oliver leaned in closer, his eyes scanning the blueprint. The familiar scent of sawdust clung to him, a testament to the hours spent in his workshop, crafting with hands that now trembled with barely contained rage. This wasn't a piece of wood he could shape or mend; this was life and death. They had called the sheriff and reported Ava and Daniel missing and told him they believed they might have been kidnapped and perhaps were being held at the old mill. Sherriff Coleman had answered that he couldn't do much about it if there were nothing more to go on. It was private property owned by a family that lived in the next town over. So, Lisa and Oliver knew they had to go there alone, even if they risked getting arrested for trespassing. They needed to know. And if it turned out that Daniel and Ava were there, they needed to give the sheriff the proof so he could take over from there and help them.

"We need to be careful of the basement," Oliver said, his voice steady despite the storm brewing within. "It's a maze down there."

Once the plan was laid bare on the kitchen table, they turned to the next phase—preparation. Their home became a command center; adrenaline-laced tension mixed with the scent of coffee that had long since gone cold.

Lisa opened a black duffel bag and revealed its contents: rope, flashlights, and a first-aid kit.

"These might come in handy," she murmured, her gaze never leaving the bag as if she could will it to contain all the answers they needed.

"Here," Oliver returned, setting down a hefty crowbar with a thud. "Just in case we need to make our own entrance."

"Or our own exit," Lisa added, a steely note in her voice.

They suited up in dark clothing and practical boots and equipped themselves with tools that felt foreign yet necessary. Lisa caught her reflection in the hallway mirror, hardly recognizing the woman staring back. A hardened resolve had replaced her warm smile, and her hair was pulled back into a no-nonsense ponytail.

"Are we ready?" Oliver asked, meeting Lisa's gaze. His hand reached for hers, an anchor amidst the chaos.

"As we'll ever be," Lisa replied, squeezing his hand in return. She had called Maggie, who had come to take the children to her place, no questions asked. She thought of Daniel's laugh, the sound that had once filled the house and now left an aching void. They would bring him back. They had to.

"Let's bring my boy home," Oliver said, his voice cracking just slightly before he composed himself once again.

They were scared, yes, but beneath that fear lay something far stronger: love, the kind that could move mountains, cross oceans, and face down the darkest of foes. It was heartwarming and exciting, thrilling and suspenseful—the kind of love that could save life. And tonight, it would have to.

Moonlight draped the small town in a silver glow as Lisa and Oliver slipped out of the house, their shadows merging with the dark contours of the sleeping buildings. They moved with silent urgency, each step carefully placed to avoid loose gravel and creaky boards that might betray their presence. The night was still, save for the occasional hoot of an owl or the rustle of wind through the leaves.

The adrenaline coursing through Lisa's veins sharpened her senses, amplifying every sound and magnifying every movement. Oliver led them through alleys he knew by heart, past the old church, and down the forgotten paths where children once played but now lay deserted.

The building loomed ahead, a monolith of brick and broken windows that seemed to swallow the darkness whole. Lisa's intimate knowledge of its layout was their advantage.

As they neared the entrance, Lisa's hand instinctively went to the small canister clipped to her belt—the pepper spray felt cold against her palm, a reminder of the danger they were about to face. She glanced back at Oliver, finding a silent promise in his determined gaze and the gun at his side. They would do whatever it took.

She paused at the door, her other hand reaching out to touch the splintered wood, feeling for vibrations, signs of life within. Her intuition screamed that they were not alone, that eyes watched them even now from the shadows. With one last deep breath, she pushed the door open and stepped into the abyss with

Oliver right behind her, a duo of hearts beating against the silence of the night.

❧

The door creaked on its hinges, an ominous sound that echoed through the stale air of the abandoned building. Lisa's heart was pounding hard in her chest as they made their entry, the darkness enveloping them like a cloak. She could feel Oliver's presence, a comforting solidity at her back.

They had barely taken two steps when the dim glow from a cracked overhead light revealed the first of their adversaries. The kidnappers, entrenched in the illusion of security, were jolted into alertness by the intrusion—a quartet of burly silhouettes rising from a dilapidated card table littered with empty beer cans and dog-eared playing cards.

"Who the hell?" one of the figures began, but the duo's swift action cut short the sentence.

Lisa's instincts kicked in; she darted forward, pepper spray in hand, unleashing a fiery stream into the eyes of the nearest man. He howled in agony, clutching his face as he stumbled back, knocking over a chair in his blind panic.

Oliver was a flurry of movement beside her. His past on the ocean had honed his reflexes, and with the grace of a seasoned fisherman battling the sea, he swung a heavy flashlight like a club, connecting with a thug's wrist. The sound of cracking bone was drowned out by the man's cry of pain as his weapon clattered to the floor.

The room erupted into chaos. A table overturned, spilling paraphernalia across the grimy floor. Shouts and curses filled the space as the kidnappers scrambled to regroup, their plans upended by the ferocity of the unexpected attack.

Lisa ducked a wild swing from one of the men, her body moving with a dancer's rhythm learned from years of protecting herself and her children. With precision, she drove her knee into his gut, using his moment of weakness to snatch the handgun from his grasp and toss it out of reach.

"Daniel!" she called out amidst the bedlam, her voice both a battle cry and a beacon of hope. "Ava?"

Through the melee, Lisa's gaze locked onto a door at the far end of the room. It was slightly ajar, a sliver of light escaping from within, beckoning them with the promise of finding Daniel and Ava.

Adrenaline surged through her veins as she fought her way toward it, Oliver right behind her, a seamless unit of determination and grit. They moved together, their bond strengthened by the peril that united them.

In that charged moment, as fist met flesh and courage stood tall against fear, Lisa knew that they were not just fighting for Ava and Daniel's freedom—they were fighting for their lives, their town, and the very essence of family that bound them all together. Oliver pulled his gun, which made them back off, at least for a bit.

The door groaned on its hinges as Lisa shouldered it open, her breaths shallow but determined. The room beyond was a stark contrast to the chaos they had left behind—a quiet chamber illuminated by a single bulb that swayed gently in some unfelt breeze. There, in the corner, Daniel huddled against the wall, his tiny frame curled into a ball of fear.

"Mommy?" His voice was a soft whimper, barely audible over the pounding of Lisa's heart.

She turned and saw Ava. She was tied up, her head slumped against her chest. She wasn't asleep. She was unconscious. Lisa ran to her and lifted her head, touching blood on the side of her hair. Lots of blood. Seeing this, she looked up at Oliver. "We need to get her to the hospital quickly."

A sudden movement caught her eye—the shadow of a man stepping out from behind the door with a raised gun. Time slowed as Lisa's instincts took over. With no thought for her own safety, she launched herself toward Daniel, wrapping her arms protectively around the boy just as the trigger clicked and a bullet sang past, embedding itself into the wall where he had been seconds before.

"Lisa!" Oliver's alarmed cry sliced through the tension.

"Keep them busy!" Lisa yelled, her voice laced with urgency.

With an understanding glance, Oliver charged at the gunman, his tall frame casting a menacing shadow.

He feinted left, then right, his movements honed by years of battling the unpredictable sea.

"Go!" Oliver bellowed, his eyes locking onto Lisa's for a fraction of a second, conveying a world of trust and shared purpose. "Take Daniel. I'll get Ava!"

Cradling Daniel against her chest, Lisa moved with a mother's ferocity, darting around the flailing bodies and dodging the wild swings aimed at Oliver. Her heart raced, each beat a drum of survival as she navigated the labyrinthine building, her every sense attuned to the precious burden in her arms.

"Almost out, Daniel. Hold on," she coaxed, feeling his small fingers clutching at her shirt.

Behind her, the cacophony of grunts and shattering glass faded into the background as she focused solely on the path ahead. Each step was a dance between life and death, and Lisa performed it with a grace born from love and desperation.

Sweat traced the contours of Lisa's face as she darted through the dim corridors, Daniel's weight a constant reminder of what was at stake. The shadows around them seemed to pulse with danger, but there was no turning back. Oliver's footsteps reverberated behind her, a steady drumbeat against the haunting echo of their pursuers' shouts. She turned around briefly and saw him running with Ava slumped over his shoulder, her weight slowing him down.

"Left, up ahead!" Oliver's voice cut through the tension, a light guiding them through the maze of uncertainty.

Lisa turned sharply, nearly losing her footing on

the slick concrete floor. The air was thick with the stench of mildew and fear. She could hear Daniel's labored breathing, each inhale a quiet plea for safety.

"Keep moving," she whispered, more to herself than to the boy in her arms. Her muscles screamed, but her resolve was ironclad. They were a team, a family forged from trials by fire, and she would see them through this.

A shadow loomed ahead. A figure stepped out from an alcove, his silhouette menacing in the scant light. The glint of metal—a weapon—sent a jolt of panic through Lisa's veins. Time slowed as the kidnapper raised his arm, aiming directly at her.

"Mommy," Daniel whimpered, his small voice piercing the thick cloud of dread. "I want my mommy."

Instinct took over. With a surge of adrenaline, Lisa twisted to the side, shielding Daniel with her body. The kidnapper lunged, and she dropped Daniel, who stood to his feet, staring at her, paralyzed. Lisa met the attacker with unexpected force. She gripped his wrist, leveraging her momentum, and twisted.

The weapon clattered to the ground.

"Run!" she roared, the sound primal and fierce.

Oliver sprang forward, barreling into the kidnapper. Their struggle was a blur of limbs and desperation. Lisa scooped up Daniel, cradling him close as she sprinted toward the exit.

Oliver grappled with the kidnapper, his movements fueled by a love so deep it left no room for hesitation.

"Lisa!" Oliver's cry spurred her on. "Keep going."

With a final effort, Oliver drove his knee into the assailant's midsection. He doubled over, gasping for breath. Oliver seized the moment, wrenching his arm behind his back, and he hit him in the back of his head with the handle of the gun until he collapsed, subdued.

"Go, go, go!" he ordered, not daring to look back as he grabbed Ava from the floor and bolted after Lisa and Daniel.

They spilled out into the night, the cool air a balm to their burning lungs. The town slept unaware, its quaint streets a jarring contrast to the chaos they had just escaped. They were alive, whole, and together.

"Let's not stop until we're home," Lisa panted.

"Home," Oliver echoed, his voice a mix of exhaustion and elation. "And then we call the sheriff, okay?"

"Deal."

Together, they raced through the darkness, leaving behind the nightmare that had ensnared them, propelled by the sheer force of their united hearts.

The key turned in the lock with a welcome click, and the door swung open to a world that seemed both familiar and forever altered. Lisa stepped into the dimly lit foyer of their home, her arm instinctively tightening around Daniel's small shoulders as Oliver followed close behind with Ava, who was waking up now but not yet fully aware of her surroundings.

Every shadow seemed to dance with the flicker of memories, each corner of the room holding echoes of laughter and whispers of danger now past. But as they moved through the silent house, it was not the shadows that took shape but the love and resilience that had brought them back to this place of refuge.

"Home," Daniel murmured, his voice laced with weariness and wonder. In response, Lisa squeezed him gently, her heart swelling with a cocktail of relief and protectiveness. The three other kids spent the night at Maggie's and would know nothing of what had happened once they got back—only that Daniel and Ava were back, and they were safe.

"We need to get you to the hospital," Oliver said, looking at Ava, who he had sat down on the couch. She groaned and looked at him, then shook her head. "No hospital. No police. Please."

"Why not? What are you afraid of?"

She shook her head with a moan and held a hand to the wound. "They hit me with a pipe or something. It will heal. I'm okay."

"Who were these people, Ava? We deserve to know."

Her eyes met his as the room held its breath, waiting for answers. Lisa stared at her, holding Daniel's hand in hers.

"I used to work for them," Ava said with a deep sigh. "When I came across something I shouldn't have. A young woman, one of my colleagues at the bar we worked at, was dead. They had killed her."

"Who had?" Oliver said. "What are you talking about?"

"The girls there. They used them to smuggle drugs across the border to Canada in fake stomachs. They'd make them look pregnant, wearing these bodysuits. But they had drugs inside them—pills, coke, you name it. This girl told them she was done working for them. She had a kid at home and couldn't risk it. So, they killed her. I happened to see them do it in my boss' office. It was an accident that I saw it. They caught me and told me to take over the girl's job, or they'd do the same to me. So, I had to travel with drugs for several years, until one day, one snoopy agent at the airport put his hand on my stomach and realized it was made of rubber. I was taken into custody, and they told me I could get a lesser punishment if I gave them names. So, I did. For Daniel's sake, so he would have a mother growing up. But I was still charged with drug smuggling, and then these people whose names I had mentioned were after me, too. So, I ran away. I knew I had to get out of there quickly. The only place I could think of was here. Back when everything was good and safe in my life. When I was with you."

Oliver exhaled deeply and rubbed his hair. "That explains a lot, Ava," he said. "I wish you would have told me this from the beginning."

"I'm sorry."

Oliver nodded. "I'm sure you are. But right now, I'll call the sheriff and tell him to go to the old mill. They might need you to testify that you were held there. Would you be able to?"

Ava had tears spring to her eyes. She swallowed, then nodded. "Y-yes."

Oliver smiled gently. "That's good. That's really brave of you."

Oliver grabbed the phone and walked away with it pressed against his ear. He returned a few minutes later. "Sheriff Coleman says that they can arrest them for trespassing. They had no right to be at the old mill. And, if we're lucky, these guys will have other warrants out for their arrests, so they won't need you. At least not yet. But he told you to remain ready just in case."

"That's a relief," Ava said.

Oliver then walked to Daniel and knelt in front of him.

"Let's get you cleaned up, buddy," he said, his eyes tracing the streaks of dirt on Daniel's face before he glanced at Lisa, his gaze conveying an ocean of unspoken thoughts. He still missed the sea and the freedom of the waves, but right now, the solid ground beneath their feet felt like the most precious treasure.

"Daddy's going to make everything okay," Oliver assured, brushing his fingers through Daniel's tousled hair. His eyes, which had seen so much pain, shone with a resilient spark.

As Oliver drew a bath for Daniel and Lisa cleaned Ava's wound, the comforting sound of running water filled the house, washing away the last remnants of fear. Lisa helped Ava prepare a warm meal; the simple act of slicing bread and ladling soup into bowls was a balm to their jangled nerves. They exchanged glances,

a silent agreement that they were more than just indi-
viduals; they were a unit bound by the ordeal they had
endured together.

Later, as they sat around the kitchen table in the
soft glow of the overhead light, the town's response
was already beginning to manifest outside their
windows. Neighbors arrived, some with covered
dishes, others with quiet offers of help. Maggie had
made sure to let them all know what had happened
after Lisa had confided in her. With its intimate web
of lives and stories, the small town closed ranks
around them, providing a shield of community spirit
and support.

"Looks like we're having a potluck," Oliver joked,
trying to ease the tension that still clung to the room
like morning fog. His laugh, though strained, was met
with grateful smiles.

"Thank you all," Lisa said when they gathered at
the door, accepting casseroles and words of encouragement. "We couldn't have gotten through this
without you." She meant every word, her gratitude as
deep as the roots of the towering oaks lining their
street.

"Anything for our own," Mr. Jenkins, the elderly
grocer, declared, his voice firm despite his advanced
years. "You folks are family."

As night settled over the town, warmth was spilling
from each window of the house into the darkness.
Inside, Lisa watched Oliver tuck Daniel into bed, the
little boy clinging to his father. Ava stood by the door-

way, her silhouette framed by the soft light, a portrait of strength and grace.

Lisa joined her, their hands finding each other, gripping tightly in mutual understanding. They were survivors, warriors who had fought back against the darkness. In this moment of calm, the healing began —slowly and tenderly—as they knit themselves back into the fabric of life, supported by the town that had become their fortress, their sanctuary. And as silence wrapped around them like a protective cloak, Lisa knew that no matter what secrets the future held, they would face them together. For in this small town where hearts beat in unison, hope was a currency that never lost its value, and love was the ultimate shield against the night's chill.

Outside, a cool breeze whispered through the town, rustling the leaves in a comforting susurration. Inside the cozy living room, Lisa and Oliver sat side by side on the worn sofa that had become their command center throughout the recent turmoil. The walls around them hummed with the quiet energy of a day winding down, yet within their clasped hands was an electric current of shared purpose.

"Look at us," Lisa murmured, her voice a blend of wonder and resolve. "We've been through a storm and come out on the other side—together."

Oliver's thumb gently stroked the back of her hand, his touch grounding. "I used to think the ocean was the only place where I could find peace. Turns out it's right here with you and the kids."

The room was cloaked in the soft glow of a single lamp, casting long shadows that danced across the floor. It felt as if the whole world had narrowed to this singular point of light, where fear and hope collided, birthing something new and tenacious.

"Once everything settles down," Lisa started, her wavy brown hair falling over her shoulder as she leaned into Oliver, "we should take a trip. I don't care where to; anywhere would be nice."

"Sounds perfect," he replied, his voice laced with anticipation. "But for now, let's just enjoy the peace and quiet."

"Where?" she asked with a grin. "With all these children here, there's no peace nor quiet anywhere."

"You think it was wrong of me to offer for Daniel to stay here until his mom gets on her feet?" he asked.

Lisa laughed. "No! I love Daniel. I was just messing with you. We do have a lot of kids, and peace and quiet are rare around here, you must admit. That doesn't mean it's bad or that I don't love it."

Lisa raised her eyes to meet his, seeing in them the reflection of her own determination. It was a look that spoke of shared battles and victories yet to come—a silent vow that they would weather any storm, no matter how fierce.

"Agreed," he replied, his heart swelling with an emotion so potent it threatened to spill over. "Our love, this family—it's stronger than any challenge we might encounter."

Their gazes locked, unspoken promises passing between them like sacred pacts. They were two souls, tempered by adversity, bound by a love that had proven itself unbreakable against the forces that sought to divide them.

With the night deepening outside their window, the small town continued its slumber, oblivious to the quiet revolution taking place within these four walls. Lisa and Oliver, their spirits intertwined, faced the unknown future not with trepidation but with a blazing, unquenchable hope.

For in their hearts, they carried the undying flame of a romance forged in the heat of danger, steeled by the cold touch of fear and now glowing with the warm promise of tomorrow.

The golden hues of the setting sun spilled through the window, casting a warm glow over the wooden tables of the café. Lisa brushed a loose strand of hair behind her ear as she sat across from Oliver, their hands clasped tightly atop the checkered tablecloth that had seen better days. The silence between them was thick, charged with the weight of recent events.

"Oliver," Lisa began, her voice shaky but laced with resolve, "Ava leaving… it's… I know you probably miss her, and so does Daniel, but I feel like we're on solid ground now. You, me, and the kids—we're a team."

Oliver's eyes, which often held a playful glint, were serious as he squeezed her hand. "I know. Ava being back in town dredged up a lot, but Lisa, you are my present and my future."

The scent of fresh coffee lingered in the air, a comforting reminder of the life they were building.

Yet, the walls of their dream shared space with the unspoken fear of failure. They had to turn things around somehow.

"Let's ask the town for help and let them know we're still here, fighting for our café. We're not alone; it's not a failure to ask for support," Lisa's voice grew bolder with each word. Oliver nodded, his determination mirroring hers.

The next morning, Lisa stepped outside as the townspeople strolled past the windows adorned with hand-carved trinkets and the promise of a warm muffin. She took a deep breath, feeling the chill of the Alaskan air invigorate her spirit. One by one, she approached the familiar faces—faces creased with lines of hardship and smiles alike.

"Morning, Joe. How's Ellen doing?" she asked, her genuine concern opening doors to conversations that wove through the struggles of running their small businesses. She shared candidly, not just as an entrepreneur, but as a neighbor—a friend.

"Times have been tough at the café and woodshop," she admitted to Mary, the postmistress, who always had a kind word for everyone. "But we're committed to making it work. We will need your support, though. We need everyone's support."

Word spread like wildfire, igniting a spark of community spirit that hadn't been felt for some time. Offers of help poured in, from flyers designed by the local high school art class to volunteer shifts covered by retirees with stories as rich as the coffee they'd serve.

"Lisa, put me down for Thursdays," boomed Big Pete, his frame dwarfing the doorway as he offered his burly hands for more than just lifting spirits.

"Can I teach a knitting circle here?" Mrs. Hadley proposed, envisioning the corner by the fireplace filled with the clack of needles and gentle gossip. We will need lots of coffee and muffins."

"Let's get those ads running in the paper," said Tom, the town's weekly gazette editor, already drafting a headline that would draw in crowds.

The heartwarming wave of support eclipsed the shadows of doubt that had crept into Lisa's mind. Her heart swelled as she realized the depth of their connection to this town—to these people who were as much a part of their story as the very wood and stone that built their establishment.

That evening, Lisa and Oliver stood side by side at the café window, watching as dusk embraced their little corner of the world. They didn't need words to express the gratitude that flowed between them or the thrill of knowing they weren't alone in their fight. Their hands found each other once again, fingers entwined with the strength of unity and the warmth of love rekindled amidst the embers of a community that refused to let them burn out.

The hum of excitement buzzed through the café as Lisa draped bunting across the ceiling beams, its colors vibrant against the warm wood. With his shirt sleeves rolled up to his elbows, Oliver arranged an array of hand-crafted wooden pieces on makeshift display tables, each a testament to his dedication and skill.

"Looks fantastic, doesn't it?" Lisa's voice was tinged with a mix of pride and nervous anticipation as she stepped back to admire their work. The café had been transformed into a festive nexus of community spirit, ready for the townspeople to gather and celebrate their renewed commitment.

"Better than fantastic," Oliver replied, his eyes catching hers with that familiar spark of shared dreams. He couldn't help but chuckle when he saw their special promotion sign, "Buy a coffee, get a story." It was their playful nod to the tales shared around their tables, the fabric of local life woven through every cup served.

Lisa's heartbeat quickened as the door chime heralded the arrival of their first guests of the day. Would their efforts be enough? The question was whispered in her mind, swiftly silenced by the smiles and cheers that greeted them. The shop brimmed with neighbors, each eager to support and indulge in the discounted offerings.

"Your craftsmanship is truly a sight to behold, Oliver," Mrs. Hadley said, admiring a delicately turned bowl.

"Thank you," he replied, a flush of modest pride coloring his cheeks. "There's a bit of the ocean in each piece."

Meanwhile, Lisa found herself deep in conversation with Mr. Jacobs, the owner of the prosperous general store down the street. He leaned in, imparting wisdom gained from years of successful trading. "Diversify your suppliers, keep the inventory fresh, and always listen to what the customers are whispering about; it's invaluable insight."

"Thank you, Mr. Jacobs. We'll definitely keep that in mind," Lisa responded, scribbling notes onto a small pad she kept handy. His advice was gold dust in these trying times.

As the event unfolded, laughter and lively chatter filled the air, creating a symphony of fellowship. Lisa glanced over at Oliver, who was demonstrating the process of sanding down a piece of driftwood, his hands moving with confident grace. The crowd was captivated, hanging on his every word—the thrill of witnessing creation in action.

"Don't forget to sign up for the workshops next week," Oliver told his students as he dismissed the class.

"I've already marked the calendar," Mr. Jacobs assured him.

The evening waned, but the energy in the room did not. Each handshake, each sale, each word of encouragement was another brick in the foundation they were building. And as the last customer left, carrying away a piece of their heart in the form of aromatic coffee beans or a lovingly carved trinket, Lisa and Oliver stood in the now-quiet space, a sense of accomplishment wrapping around them like a warm blanket.

"Today was just the beginning, wasn't it?" Lisa

murmured, her gaze taking in the café they had poured their souls into.

"Only the beginning," Oliver confirmed, his arm wrapping around her shoulders.

❧

The chime above the door jingled incessantly as patrons streamed in and out of the bustling café a couple of days later, their voices blending into a symphony of community spirit. Lisa watched from behind the counter, her heart swelling with pride as she noticed the familiar faces that had become part of their extended family. The smell of freshly brewed coffee mingled with the sweet scent of homemade pastries, creating an inviting warmth that seemed to hug each customer as they entered.

"Mom, where do you want these?" Ethan asked, balancing a tray of cinnamon rolls with the focus of a tightrope walker as he navigated through the crowded space.

"Right there, sweetheart, next to the register," Lisa directed him with a grateful smile. His green eyes sparkled with determination, echoing the resilience they all shared. Abigail trailed behind him, clutching napkins meticulously folded into swans, her contribution to their homegrown charm.

Oliver emerged from the woodwork shop, his hands dusted with sawdust, carrying a newly finished oak coffee table. His presence commanded attention, yet his easy smile drew people in. "Look what we've got here," he announced, setting the piece in a prominent display. "Fresh from the workshop!"

A murmur of admiration rippled through the crowd, and Lisa could hardly believe how far they had come. Their once precarious dream was now the beating heart of the town's daily life. Customers not only came for the food and crafts but for the sense of belonging that thrived within these walls.

"Mom, can I show Mr. Jenkins the birdhouse I made?" Ethan asked, his voice trembling with excitement.

"Of course, go ahead." Lisa nodded, watching as her son confidently approached their neighbor from across the street, a bird enthusiast. She caught Oliver's eye, and they exchanged a glance that spoke volumes. They were doing more than running a business; they were crafting a legacy.

Abigail, meanwhile, flitted between tables, her laughter a melody that lifted spirits. She handed out her napkin creations, leaving behind smiles brighter than the Alaskan summer sun.

"Everything looks wonderful, you two," said Martha, an elderly regular, as she sipped her tea. "You've built something special here."

"Thank you, Martha. It means a lot coming from you," Lisa replied, her voice thick with emotion. It wasn't just about the thriving business or the renewed vigor with which they approached each day—it was about this: the bond between them and their beloved townspeople.

"Hey, Oliver, let me help you with those orders,"

Ethan called out, already donning an apron too big for his slender frame. Beside him, Abigail arranged cookies on a plate with artistic flair, her small fingers working with surprising adeptness.

"Looks like you're raising quite the entrepreneurs," Chuck, the postman, chuckled as he collected his regular order of black coffee and a sandwich.

"More like they're raising us at times," Oliver responded with a wink. And it was true—in teaching their children, they were learning anew the values of hard work, persistence, and hope.

Amidst the crescendo of crickets and the soft rustling of leaves, two silhouettes moved harmoniously under the vast Alaskan sky. Lisa's breath came in short bursts as she matched Oliver's stride, their boots crunching on the gravelly path that led up Mount Verity. The thrill of adventure pulsed through her veins—a sensation she hadn't felt since long before the café became their world.

"Race you to the top," Oliver teased, his eyes twinkling with a challenge.

"Oliver Thompson, are you trying to kill me?" Lisa laughed, but the spark in her gaze said she was already accepting the dare.

They picked up the pace, their laughter mingling with the wind until they reached the peak. There, gazing out over the sprawling wilderness, they found solace in each other's embrace, the fiery hues of the sunset reflecting the renewed passion in their relationship.

"Beautiful, isn't it? Just like you," Oliver whispered into her hair, his lips brushing against her temple tenderly.

Lisa leaned back to meet his gaze, her heart swelling. "I love our date nights," she admitted. "They remind me of us—of why we fight so hard for everything."

"Me too," he agreed, sealing his words with a kiss that bridged the gap between struggle and serenity.

Their descent was less about the race and more about connection; hands clasped, sharing dreams and whispers of the future.

Back home, the warmth of family life embraced them. Daniel sat at the kitchen table, diligently drawing, his tongue peeking out in concentration. His latest masterpiece depicted the front of the café, with stick figures holding hands.

"Look, Lisa!" he exclaimed, rushing forward to present his artwork. "It's you and Oliver and me and Ethan and Abigail! We're all together! Julia is inside, sleeping in her crib."

Lisa scooped him up, noting the careful inclusion of every family member. "This is wonderful, Daniel. You've made us all so happy being here with us," she said, her voice thick with emotion.

"Really?" Daniel's eyes were wide, hopeful.

"Absolutely," Oliver chimed in, affectionately ruffling the boy's hair. "You're part of this family and always will be."

"Always and forever," Lisa said.

That night, after tucking the children into bed, Lisa and Oliver lingered in the hallway as they listened to the soft breathing of the newest member of their family.

"Today was perfect," Lisa murmured, her head resting against Oliver's shoulder.

"Every day is perfect as long as I'm with you." Oliver's voice was resolute, his promise echoing in the quiet space between heartbeats.

Chapter Sixteen

The door creaked open, its familiar groan a symphony, as Lisa stepped over the threshold with Oliver close behind. The cool, shadow-laden air of their small bedroom wrapped around them like a protective shroud, erasing the lines of stress that had etched themselves across their faces during the day's business at the café. Lisa's chest heaved with each breath, her wavy brown hair framing her face in disarray—a stark contrast to the warm smile that now timidly played on her lips. Relief flushed her cheeks as she drank in the sight of their sanctuary.

Oliver's tall frame filled the doorway for a moment before he pushed the door shut with a definitive click. His dark hair was tousled, and his charming smile, though worn, was no less captivating. It mirrored the gratitude shining in his eyes—eyes that reflected the moonlight streaming through the window, giving him an almost ethereal glow.

For a silent, suspended moment, they simply stood

there, their gazes locked, each reading the other's soul like an open book. The intensity of the day's workload still hung heavily between them, a tangible thread woven into the fabric of their joined lives. Then, without a word, they moved toward each other, driven by an instinctive need for connection, for affirmation. Oliver looked into her eyes, and her heart melted. He grabbed both her hands in his.

Then he dropped down on one knee, his body shaking, tears welling up in his eyes. He opened the box and presented her with the ring he had been carrying around for weeks now, waiting for the right moment. And it was now. He just knew it in his heart.

"L-Lisa?"

She sniffled, pushing back tears that had sprung to her eyes when she saw him holding the ring. "Yes, Oliver?"

"W-will you marry me? Will you make me the happiest man in the world?"

She wiped away a tear that had escaped, then smiled heartfelt. "Yes, Oliver. I would love to marry you."

Their embrace was a collision of emotions, a fusion of heartwarming triumph over the trials they had weathered. Lisa's arms wound around Oliver's waist, her fingers gripping the fabric of his shirt as if to anchor herself in the reality of his presence. Oliver's arms encased her with equal fervor, and the muscles that had once hoisted nets on his fishing boat now provided a different kind of strength.

They held each other, bodies pressed so close that

the line where one ended and the other began blurred into insignificance. Their hearts beat in a shared rhythm, a silent language of love and mutual appreciation flowing through them. Time seemed to stretch and bend, allowing them this stolen moment of serenity amidst the chaos of their lives.

In this quiet space, there was no need for words; their embrace said everything. Promise, hope, and the thrill of overcoming adversity infused their touch, binding them closer than ever. Oliver's chin rested atop Lisa's head, his senses filled with the scent of her —home and hearth and something indefinably her. And Lisa, her vigilant guard lowered for now, allowed herself to lean fully into the man who had become her partner not only in business but in life, trusting him with the weight of her world.

Their embrace was both an ending and a beginning—the closing of one chapter of suspense and the opening of another, where the thrills would be of their own making, crafted with love and the determination to forge ahead, hand in hand.

They turned to each other once more with a shared glance that spoke volumes. There was no need for words as they slipped beneath the cool sheets of their bed, the fabric whispering across their skin in welcome. Oliver wrapped his arms around Lisa, pulling her close until she was nestled against his chest, her heartbeat a steady drum against his own.

Their bodies entwined, a tangle of limbs and shared warmth, and they lay in silence. Here, in the quiet intimacy of their room, the thrills and suspense of the day's events transformed into a heartwarming sense of completeness. Every brush of skin, every breath they shared, wove them tighter together, fortifying the bond that recent trials had only strengthened.

§

Lisa smoothed the fabric of her dress, the soft lace whispering against her fingertips. Her heart thrummed with a cocktail of excitement and nerves as she stepped onto the sun-dappled clearing that had been transformed into an outdoor chapel, their very own slice of paradise nestled in the small town they called home.

Oliver stood at the altar, his dark hair tousled just enough to give him that roguishly handsome look that always caught her breath. He turned, and their eyes met across the distance. The world seemed to pause, the gentle rustle of leaves and distant birds chirping the only sounds in the otherwise hushed reverence of the moment.

Their children, Ethan, carrying Julia, Abigail, and Daniel, flanked her, beaming with pride. Together, they walked down the aisle, symbolizing their united front, a family woven from strands of love and resilience. Lisa's gaze never wavered from Oliver's, the unspoken promises they had made to each other echoing in the space between them.

As Lisa reached Oliver's side, he extended his hand, his touch grounding her. They turned to face one another, and it was as if the gathering of friends and family faded away, leaving only the two of them standing on the cusp of forever.

"Lisa," Oliver began, his voice clear and strong, "I used to think the ocean was my greatest love—its vastness, its mystery, its constant dance with the shore. But then I met you, and suddenly, I found a depth that surpassed any sea. You are my safe harbor, my true north, and today, I promise to be yours. Through every storm and every calm, I will stand by your side."

Tears glistened in Lisa's eyes as the warmth of his words washed over her. "Oliver," she replied, her voice steady with the weight of her emotion, "life has taught me to be cautious, but with you, I've learned to trust again. You and the kids are the melody to my song, the anchor to my soul. I vow to cherish our love, nurture it, and always remember that together, we are stronger than apart. No matter what twists and turns lie ahead, we will navigate them, hand in hand, heart in heart."

A hush fell upon the gathering as they exchanged rings, simple bands that glimmered in the sunlight—a testament to the beauty in simplicity, the strength in unity.

"By the power vested in me, I now pronounce you husband and wife." The officiant's voice rang out, full of joy and solemnity. "You may kiss the bride."

Their kiss sealed their vows, a tender collision of lips that spoke volumes more than any words could. Cheers erupted around them, a symphony of happiness that echoed through the trees and into the bright blue expanse above.

As they turned to face their loved ones, hands clasped tightly, the suspense of what lay ahead intermingled with the thrill of the present. They had weathered storms before, and there would be more on the horizon, but as they stepped forward into their shared future, the overwhelming sense of love and support from their community wrapped around them like a protective embrace.

They were embarking on the greatest adventure of all—a lifetime of love, challenges, and triumphs.

And they were ready. Come what may.

THE END

Are you desperate to find out what happens to Lisa and Oliver next?
Get the third heart warming and captivating installment in the series, ***A Sister's Secret*** on Amazon.com or read on for an **exclusive excerpt...**

A Sister's Secret

〜〜〜

AN EXCERPT

INTRODUCTION

"Newly married, Oliver and Lisa are having the time of their lives in their small Alaskan town. The kids are thriving, and so is the family business. The café and woodshop are everything Oliver and Lisa dreamt of, and they almost believe they have it all.
Until their world is shattered by the news of Oliver's sister's death.
Death by suicide, the police say."

This book will have you turning the pages late into the night"

Chapter One

The golden glow of the setting sun spilled through the sheer curtains, casting a warm hue across the living room where laughter bubbled like a brook in springtime. Daniel was seated cross-legged on the floor, constructing an intricate fortress from wooden blocks, his brow furrowed in concentration. With her curly brown hair bouncing with each giggle, Abigail maneuvered her doll to be the fortress's queen, commanding it with a high-pitched voice that was all authority and mirth. Ethan had joined in, too, even though he felt he was too old to play anymore. Being with his younger siblings often persuaded him to reconnect with his inner child anyway—for their sake, of course. Because they always begged him to join them. And cradled in Lisa's arms, little Julia cooed softly, her tiny fingers wrapped around one of Lisa's, anchoring herself to the heart of the family.

Lisa glanced up from Julia to find Oliver watching

them, his blue eyes tender and soft around the edges, as if the scene before him were a painting he wished to preserve forever. He knelt beside Daniel, who had just turned six, offering a block to fortify the ramparts and winking at Lisa over his son's head. It was a simple gesture, yet it spoke volumes of the love and solidarity that had become the foundation of their blended family.

"Smells like dinner's ready," Oliver murmured, his voice low and resonant. The scent of freshly baked bread wafted through the house, a testament to the hours spent in the kitchen, hands dusted with flour, shoulders brushing, as they prepared their meal together.

"Come on, kiddos, let's wash up!" Lisa announced, her tone infused with the anticipation of the feast awaiting them.

Daniel reluctantly abandoned his fortress while Abigail scooped up her doll, declaring that royalty must dine as well. Together, they scampered toward the bathroom, their footsteps light and carefree.

In the dining room, the table was set with mismatched plates and cutlery that told stories of past lives and new beginnings. Each chair was pulled out, waiting to be filled with the warmth of familial love. As they gathered, Ethan took it upon himself to help Julia into her high chair, his protective instincts always at the forefront despite his tender age. The baby's legs protested being restrained since she just learned to walk.

They sat, hand in hand, forming an unbroken circle around the table laden with dishes that steamed with promise.

"Can I say grace?" Abigail asked, her small voice earnest in the quiet that had settled over them.

"Of course, sweetheart," Lisa said, squeezing Oliver's hand—a silent thank you for the peace they'd found in each other.

Abigail's words were a simple expression of gratitude for the food, their safety, and, most of all, for being together. As they echoed "Amen" in unison, a sense of fulfillment swept through Lisa, a thrilling rush from knowing they had weathered storms to reach this harbor of joy. The golden crust of the homemade bread broke with a satisfying crunch under Lisa's knife, releasing a yeasty cloud that mingled with the aroma of roasted vegetables and seasoned chicken.

"Let's eat!" Oliver declared, and the spell was broken, replaced by the clatter of serving spoons and the chatter of children eager to share the events of their day.

As they passed dishes and poured drinks, laughter again filled the room, weaving a tapestry of contentment that hung tangibly in the air. Lisa caught Oliver's gaze and held it, a silent conversation passing between them—one of resilience, shared dreams, and the unspoken thrill of navigating life's journey together.

Lisa's hands moved with practiced ease, dusted lightly with flour as she slid a batch of cinnamon swirl scones into the oven. The warmth from the open flame brushed against her cheeks, a comforting reminder of the many mornings spent perfecting recipes that now tempted the townsfolk into their cozy establishment. Oliver, his sleeves rolled up to his elbows, was at the other end of the café, meticulously sanding the edges of a cedar coffee table he had been working on for weeks. The rhythmic sound of the sandpaper against the wood was a soothing backdrop to the murmur of customers.

"Morning, Lisa!" Mrs. Dalton called out, stepping inside with the bell above the door chiming her arrival. "I swear, the whole town can smell your baking today!"

"Good morning, Marjorie," Lisa replied, her voice laced with pride. "I hope it tastes as good as it smells."

"It always does, dear," Mrs. Dalton said, her eyes twinkling as she eyed the display case.

Around them, the café hummed with life. Locals sat in mismatched chairs at tables Oliver had lovingly restored, each telling its own story. The air was alive with the clink of coffee cups and the soft laughter of patrons who came not only for the food and furniture but for the atmosphere that Lisa and Oliver had cultivated—a blend of rustic charm and heartfelt hospitality.

"Oliver, this piece is stunning," Mr. Jenkins, the local librarian, remarked, running a hand over the smooth grain of the table. "You've truly outdone yourself."

"Thanks, Sam," Oliver responded, his eyes lighting up with the compliment. He looked across the room at Lisa, sharing a smile that spoke volumes. They were more than business partners; they were artisans of their own future, building it with every cake baked and every piece of wood shaped.

As the morning gave way to afternoon, the ebb and flow of customers remained steady. Tourists, drawn by word-of-mouth recommendations, snapped photos of the woodwork and savored the homemade pastries. Lisa noticed how they lingered, soaking in the ambiance, reluctant to leave the little oasis she and Oliver had created.

"Seems like we're becoming quite the spot on the map," Oliver whispered to Lisa in a rare quiet moment during the lunchtime rush.

"Only because you make this place impossible to forget," she replied, squeezing his hand.

Their connection was palpable, not just to each other but to everyone who crossed the threshold. It was as if the shop throbbed with their shared pulse—a beacon of dedication and love in the heart of a small town that had become their biggest supporter.

As the sun began its descent, casting golden hues through the front windows, Lisa caught sight of the community board brimming with flyers for events and services. Their upcoming woodworking class was already filled with sign-ups, a testament to the trust and respect they'd garnered.

"Look at this, Ollie," she said, pointing at the board. "We might need to schedule another class."

"Or two," he chuckled, the lines around his eyes crinkling with delight. The thought of teaching others their craft and passing on a piece of themselves was both thrilling and a touch daunting. Oliver never liked being in front of a crowd much, but it was easier with Lisa by his side.

The day wound down with the last customer leaving with a satisfied sigh and a promise to return. As Lisa turned the sign to "Closed," she leaned back against the door, capturing the scene before her—the tables filled with traces of joy, the lingering scent of coffee, and Oliver locking away his tools, his hands still bearing the evidence of hard work.

"Another day," she murmured, contentment sweeping over her.

"Another day living our dreams," Oliver agreed, crossing the room to wrap his arms around her. In this space they had carved out for themselves, amidst the sawdust and sugar, they found their haven, wrapped up in the heartwarming embrace of a community that had become their family.

The sun dipped low on the horizon, painting the town square in hues of orange and pink as Lisa and Oliver stepped into the thrum of the annual Harvest Festival. Children dashed by with painted faces and balloons while a local band filled the air with lively tunes that beckoned even the shyest toes to tap.

"Isn't this something?" Lisa beamed, her eyes reflecting the festival lights strung from lamppost to lamppost like stars brought down to earth. She felt Oliver's hand tighten around hers, an unspoken acknowledgment of their shared joy.

"Hey, there's the dynamic duo!" Mayor Johnson called out, his voice booming above the chatter as he approached them with open arms. Murmurs of affection and admiration followed their path, the couple weaving through claps on the back and warm embraces. It was clear they were more than just business owners; they were becoming the heart of the community.

"Care for a dance, milady?" Oliver teased, bowing slightly. The playful glint in his eyes revealed a side of him that flourished in these moments of carefree celebration.

Lisa laughed, the sound mingling with the music, and accepted. They swayed together amidst fellow townsfolk, sharing smiles and laughter, their movements a silent language of love. It was here, among friends and neighbors, where the thrill of belonging wrapped around them like a cherished quilt.

As the evening waned and the last song played, they reluctantly bid farewell to the festivities, promising to carry the warmth of the town's embrace back home.

The following morning, the family found themselves at the cusp of the ocean, the beach sprawling before them like an untouched canvas. Ethan, Abigail, and Daniel bolted toward the shoreline, their squeals dissolving into the rhythmic crash of waves, with Julia struggling to keep up.

"Race you to the water!" Ethan challenged, his voice hitching with excitement.

"Last one in is a rotten jellyfish!" Daniel shouted, not far behind.

"Remember to stay where we can see you!" Lisa called after them as they jumped into the cold water, squealing, but her words were swept away by the wind. She felt a chill as the breeze hit her and thought the kids had to be crazy to go in the water in September when it was only fifty degrees out. She watched as Oliver helped Abigail hoist a kite into the sky, his silhouette framed against the backdrop of endless blue, a contented sigh escaping her lips.

"Look at them," Oliver said, returning to Lisa's side, his gaze lingering on the children who were now out of the water again, building a sandcastle fortress. "This—this right here—is what life's all about."

Lisa nodded, the breeze catching strands of her wavy brown hair. She clasped Oliver's hand, feeling the grains of sand stick to her skin, a tactile reminder of the simple pleasures surrounding them.

"Let's build our own castle," she suggested, the spark of challenge in her eyes igniting a similar flame in his.

Together, they set to work, crafting turrets and

walls, their creation growing more elaborate by the minute, their laughter joining the chorus of their children's. The suspense of each wave threatening to wash away their efforts only added to the thrill, a metaphor for the life they had built—beautiful, fragile, yet resilient.

As the day gave way to the soft glow of dusk and the kites were reeled in, they stood back to admire their sandy empire, knowing the sea would soon reclaim it. But the memories, the pure, undeniable happiness etched into this moment, would remain theirs forever.

The beach trip concluded with the family gathered at the water's edge, watching the sun sink beneath the waves. Lisa leaned into Oliver, her heart brimming with gratitude.

The hum of the cafe's espresso machine fell silent, and in that quiet, Lisa caught Oliver's eye from across the room. His hands were still, resting atop a half-finished wooden sculpture that was meant to be their next big seller. The ledger was open on the counter before her, screaming a truth they both had tried to avoid: numbers still in red, margins too thin. The café was doing better than ever, but the numbers still weren't as good as they needed them to be.

"Ollie," she called softly, not wanting to worry the children who were upstairs preparing for their school play.

Oliver set down his chisel and came to her, the scent of sawdust and coffee mingling between them. "I know," he said, his voice steady despite the storm brewing in his eyes. "I've seen the books."

Lisa bit her lip, her gaze drifting back to the page. "We could… maybe cut back on some supplies—hold off on the new espresso machine?"

He nodded, wrapping an arm around her waist and pulling her close as if to physically shield her from the weight of their worries. "And I can try to sell some pieces online—expand our reach beyond the town?"

Their foreheads touched in a silent exchange of strength. "We'll make it work together," Lisa murmured, feeling the knot in her chest loosen just a little at the promise in Oliver's eyes.

"Like we always do," he replied, a half-smile breaking through.

"Mom! Oliver!" Ethan's voice echoed as he bounded down the stairs, Abigail and Daniel trailing behind him. All three were adorned in costumes vibrant with color and childish enthusiasm. Julia stumbled behind them, trying to keep up with their longer legs.

"Look at you!" Lisa exclaimed, the financial crisis momentarily forgotten.

"Is it time?" Oliver asked, glancing at his watch.

"Twenty minutes until curtain!" Ethan announced proudly, puffing out his chest.

They hurried to the school auditorium, where parents and neighbors filled the seats, buzzing with anticipation. As the lights dimmed, Lisa squeezed Oliver's hand, her heart swelling with pride.

The curtains lifted, and there they were: Ethan as the brave knight, Abigail as the clever wizard, and little Daniel, the enchanted forest creature. Their lines were delivered with adorable determination, their movements exaggerated yet endearing. The play unfolded, a whirlwind of magic and triumph, and Lisa felt her throat tighten at the sight of their children so boldly claiming their moment.

When the final bow was taken, the applause was thunderous. Lisa and Oliver were on their feet, clapping until their hands ached, whistles and cheers escaping their lips.

"Did you see Daniel's somersault?" Oliver leaned in, his voice thick with pride.

"And Abby's spell-casting? She's a natural!" Lisa beamed.

Ethan caught sight of them from the stage, his grin wide and victorious. They met backstage, enveloped in the chaos of excited children and proud parents, yet their family felt like the only people in the world.

"Did I do good?" Daniel's eyes sparkled up at Lisa.

"You were amazing, sweetheart," she said, lifting him into a hug that spoke volumes of love and reassurance. She wasn't his biological mother, but he felt closer to her with every day that passed.

"Best night ever!" Abigail declared, bouncing on the balls of her feet.

"Let's celebrate," Oliver suggested, and the idea was met with ecstatic nods.

"I have hot chocolate and cinnamon buns ready at the café," Lisa said.

As they left the auditorium, Lisa glanced at the stars beginning to pepper the night sky. Challenges would come and go, but these moments—these victories both on stage and within the walls of their home—were the true measure of their lives. Together, they walked toward the café, the children chattering excitedly, their future as bright as the constellations above.

Chapter Two

The door to the Seabreeze Café swung open with a purpose that matched the brisk Alaskan morning breeze, causing the chime above to sing its metallic greeting. Heads turned almost in unison toward the entrance as Sheriff James "Jim" Coleman stepped inside. The hum of conversation dwindled into a suspenseful silence, punctuated only by the gentle clinking of coffee cups being set down mid-sip and the soft scrape of chair legs against the wooden floor.

Oliver Thompson, his hands steady from years of coaxing shapes out of wood, felt a tremor run through them as he caught sight of the sheriff. The man's silhouette was all too familiar—a harbinger of order and, occasionally, bearer of bad tidings in their close-knit community. Oliver's pulse thudded at his temples, his heart drumming a rhythm that spoke of both anticipation and dread.

The cafe's cozy warmth did little to ease the

sudden chill that seemed to coil around Oliver's spine. He stood frozen behind the counter, his fingers tightening involuntarily around the handle of the coffee pot he'd been about to refill. His blue eyes, usually warm with laughter shared with his woodworking students or love for his family, now mirrored the stormy gray of the sea during a squall.

Sheriff Coleman's boots echoed on the hardwood floor, a staccato beat that commanded attention and respect. As he navigated through the maze of tables, the locals watched, their expressions a blend of curiosity and concern. They knew, just as Oliver did that the sheriff's presence here was no social call. It was as if the room itself held its breath, bracing for the unknown.

Oliver's grip on the coffee pot slackened, and he placed it back onto the warmer with a care that belied the turmoil brewing within him. He swallowed hard, trying to dislodge the knot that had formed in his throat. Each step the sheriff took toward him felt like a countdown, a tick-tock toward a revelation he wasn't sure he was ready to face.

"Morning, Sheriff," Oliver managed to say, his voice betraying none of the unease that swarmed like bees in his stomach. The forced smile he offered was one he had mastered over the years—a mask to hide the scars left by a family history that always seemed to loom over him like a shadow.

Sheriff Coleman nodded in acknowledgment; his stern expression softened ever so slightly by the lines of genuine concern etched around his eyes. The air was thick with unspoken words, and the café, once abuzz with the day's gossip and laughter, was now a silent witness to the palpable tension that enveloped both men.

The sheriff's boots thudded against the faded linoleum floor, a steady drum that matched the racing of Oliver's heart. He watched the man weave through the scattered chairs and tables, his towering frame cutting a path straight to the counter where Oliver stood, trapped by both expectation and dread.

"Oliver," Sheriff Coleman's voice was low, the timbre barely rising above the hum of the refrigerators in the corner. "We need to talk. Privately."

Every pair of eyes in the café seemed to burn into Oliver's back, igniting the anxiety that simmered beneath his skin. His hands gripped the edge of the counter until his knuckles blanched. There was no mistaking the seriousness etched into the lines of the sheriff's face, no escaping the urgency that laced his words.

"Of course, Sheriff," Oliver replied, his tone steadier than he felt. With a glance at the curious onlookers, he wiped his palms on his apron and rounded the counter. The familiar weight of responsibility, a constant companion since his youth, settled heavily on his shoulders as he followed the sheriff's lead.

They moved together through the narrow hallway that ran like an artery behind the cafe's public facade. Each step reverberated off the tight walls, a solemn echo to their silent procession. Oliver felt the space around him shrink, compressing the air until it became something thick and tangible.

The small office at the end of the hall was a cramped room cluttered with old filing cabinets and stacks of paperwork.

Sheriff Coleman stepped inside first, his presence dominating the confined space. Oliver entered hesitantly, the door clicking shut behind him with an ominous finality. Alone now, cut off from the outside world, the two men faced each other—each braced for the impact of words yet unspoken, each aware that whatever came next would irrevocably alter the course of the day.

&

Sheriff Coleman's hand reached up, pausing momentarily before grasping the brim of his hat. He pulled it off slowly, revealing a furrowed brow and a scalp dusted with gray. The air seemed to still in that cramped office as if it, too, anticipated the weight of what was to come.

"Oliver," he began, his voice uncharacteristically gentle, yet laden with an unmistakable sorrow. "I'm afraid I've got some bad news about your sister, Michelle."

The words hung there, suspended in the stale office air. Oliver's heart, already pounding against the walls of his chest, threatened to break free.

"My sister?" His own voice sounded foreign to him, distant and hollow. "What about her?"

"It's... she's passed away, Oliver." The sheriff's eyes, usually so steady, flickered with emotion. "I am so very sorry."

A cold tide of shock washed over Oliver's senses, dousing the embers of hope that always burned for reconciliation, for another chance to see Michelle and mend the fractures of the past. His sister was a part of his life that had been absent yet omnipresent like the shadow of a dream long forgotten upon waking.

"Passed away?" Oliver echoed, his mind recoiling, seeking refuge in denial. How could it be? Michelle, with her rebellious spirit and wild laughter, was gone? She was out there somewhere, or so he had always believed, living her life.

Memories surged through him, unbidden. Images of a young girl with braided hair, her face alight with mischief as they played along the rugged coastline. He had been a protector from childhood's squabbles and scraped knees. And then, the years peeled away to reveal darker times when their paths diverged into forests thick with silence and unspoken regrets.

"Oliver?" The sheriff's hand rested on his shoulder, grounding him to the present.

"Wh-what happened?" Oliver's words stumbled out, tripping over themselves as his thoughts raced. She had been gone so long, a whisper of a life that once ran parallel to his own. What had claimed her? Was it the wilderness she sought or something more sinister?

"Details are scarce right now," Sheriff Coleman

admitted. "But I promise you, we will find out. We owe it to her… to you."

Oliver nodded, numbness seeping into his limbs. A lifetime of questions bloomed in his chest, thorny and wild. Yet amidst the tumult of grief and confusion, one thing stood clear and unwavering: he would unearth the truth of his sister's fate, for the love that persisted through absence and silence, for the bond not even death could sever.

Lisa paused, the clink of coffee cups and murmurs from the café fading into a distant hum as she caught sight of Sheriff Coleman leaving the office and finding a seat at a nearby table. He caught Lisa's eye, and his expression seemed to give her permission to go to Oliver. The subtle furrow of her brow spoke volumes of her intuition that something was amiss. A mother's instinct, woven with threads of past adversities, honed her sensitivity to the unseen troubles lurking beneath the surface of everyday life. She wiped her hands on her apron, the fabric a testament to countless hours of nurturing and care within these walls, and moved with purpose toward the narrow hallway leading to the back office.

The door was ajar, revealing Oliver standing still as a statue, his usually warm eyes now pools of despair. Lisa's heart contracted at the sight, a silent alarm ringing through her veins. Without hesitation, she crossed the threshold, her footsteps soft but swift.

As if guided by a force greater than herself, she reached Oliver's side in an instant, her arms enfolding him with a strength forged from years of facing her own demons and emerging resilient.

"Oliver?" Her voice was gentle yet laced with concern as she held him close, feeling the tremors that shook his frame.

His voice was fractured by emotion, barely louder than a whisper. "It's Michelle… she's gone, Lisa."

The words hung between them, each syllable laden with a heartbreaking finality. Lisa's embrace tightened as she absorbed the blow of his grief, the sharp edge of loss cutting through the air.

Tears blurred her vision, empathy blooming within her like a delicate yet persistent flower pushing through winter's frost.

"Oh, Oliver, I'm so sorry," she managed to say, her voice thick with sorrow. Her hazel eyes, always so attentive and kind, now reflected the shared pain that connected their souls in this moment of raw vulnerability.

In the quiet of the office, with only the faint sounds of life continuing outside, they stood entwined by more than just their arms. Heavy with the loss of a sister he had both adored and mourned for years, Oliver's heart found a glimmer of solace in Lisa's unwavering support. And as the reality of his loss seeped into the depths of their being, they leaned on one another, finding a semblance of peace amidst the turmoil.

Sheriff Coleman's silhouette loomed in the doorway, his presence a solemn anchor in the storm of emotion that raged through the small office. The lines etching his face seemed to deepen as he took in the sight of Oliver and Lisa, their bodies interlocked in a desperate bid for comfort.

"I'm sorry to be the bearer of such news," he said, his voice a low rumble of empathy that resonated in the confined space. "Oliver, Lisa, I want you both to know that I'll turn over every stone to give you answers. We owe Michelle that much. We all loved her."

The sheriff's eyes, usually so sharp and assessing, now held a softness that belied his gruff exterior. It was clear that beneath the badge and the years of upholding law and order, Jim Coleman's heart bled just as theirs did.

Oliver nodded, his jaw clenched in an effort to stave off the swell of emotions threatening to spill forth once more. Lisa, feeling the tension in her husband's frame, drew him closer, her own grief mingling with his as they sought refuge in each other's arms.

"Thank you, Jim," Oliver managed to say, his words muffled against Lisa's hair. The café around them faded into irrelevance, the clinking of dishes and murmur of patrons nothing but a distant echo against the gravity of their loss.

Lisa's tears were silent. Her strength in this

moment manifested not through stoicism but through the tenderness with which she held Oliver.

Together, they stood, wrapped in a cocoon of shared sorrow and love. The world outside might continue its relentless march forward, but within the confines of the office, time seemed to pause, allowing them just a moment to breathe—to absorb the shock of a universe abruptly and irrevocably altered.

In the quiet aftermath of the sheriff's promise, the air buzzed with unspoken questions and fears about what lay ahead.

Chapter Three

The edges of the worn wooden table bit into Oliver's fingers as his grip tightened, a futile attempt to anchor himself against the news that had just capsized his world. The sheriff's words still echoed in the room, bouncing off walls hung with pictures of happier times, now tainted with the grief of loss.

Oliver nodded silently to Sheriff Coleman, his throat too tight to form words. He could feel the shock painted across his face, a mirror of the heartbreak he saw in Lisa's eyes.

"We should go," he finally managed. His voice was a stranger's—a hollow sound that seemed inadequate amidst the swirling emotions threatening to overwhelm him.

"Your parents are expecting us," Sheriff Coleman added gently, his stern features softened with empathy.

As they drove through town, the familiar sights blurred past Oliver and Lisa, leaving them wrapped in an oppressive silence broken only by the occasional gravel crunch beneath the tires. The sheriff's cruiser rolled to a stop outside the Thompson family home, secluded amongst the evergreens on the outskirts of their small town.

"I'll wait for you here," the sheriff said. "Give you some privacy to talk. I'll take you both home after. I already spoke with them earlier."

"Thanks, Jim," Oliver said.

"It's the least I can do. We all loved Michelle around here. She was a wild one, but we love those too."

Oliver stepped out into the biting air, its chill a stark contrast to the warmth he once felt here. His parents, John and Molly, stood waiting on the porch, their faces etched with sorrow and age, arms around each other in a rare display of unity. For a moment, it seemed as if the years of tension and unspoken regrets could be set aside, forgotten in the shadow of a shared tragedy.

"Mom, Dad," Oliver said, his voice cracking like thin ice beneath his feet.

"Oliver," Molly whispered, reaching out a hand that trembled as much from emotion as from the cold. Her gaze shifted to Lisa, offering a silent plea for understanding in these moments where words would always fall short.

They moved together, a family, broken and reassembling in the face of loss, each touch and glance a fragile thread weaving them closer. The creak of the porch underfoot punctuated their silent communion, a reminder of the many summers spent in laughter and the winters that left them isolated from one another.

As they crossed the threshold into the house, memories flooded back for Oliver—of Michelle's laughter echoing down the hallways, of arguments that left scars no winter could erase. In this space filled with both love and regret, the weight of the past pressed down upon them all, urging them to confront the secrets that had long cast shadows over their lives.

The heavy oak door closed behind them with a definitive thud, sealing Oliver, Lisa, and his parents in the living room that felt more like a mausoleum of past emotions than a place of comfort. Oliver's father, John, stood stiffly by the fireplace, his eyes flicking everywhere but at his son. Molly's hands were clasped tightly in her lap, her knuckles white with the effort as she stared at Oliver, her face a roadmap of sorrow etched deep into her skin.

"Oliver," John's voice was barely audible, a low rumble that didn't dare rise above a whisper, as if he feared what might come out if he allowed himself to speak any louder.

"Dad," Oliver replied, his own voice laden with years of words unsaid. The air crackled with tension, each breath they took seeming to stir up dust and memories best left undisturbed.

Standing beside Oliver, Lisa felt the tangible ache

of the space between father and son. She reached out, her fingers brushing against Oliver's hand, which trembled ever so slightly. He looked down at their entwined hands, and his resolve seemed to waver for a moment. But then he squeezed back, a silent message of gratitude for her presence.

Molly finally broke the silence, standing with an effort that seemed to take everything out of her.

"I made some tea," she said, her voice cracking like the thin ice on the town's lake in early winter.

"Thank you," Lisa murmured, even as she felt the hollowness of the gesture. Tea couldn't mend the fractures in this family or warm the chill that had settled in the room.

They sat around a coffee table laden with mismatched cups and a teapot that had seen better days. Oliver's gaze lifted to meet his mother's, searching for something—anything—that might bridge the gap time had carved between them. But when Molly's eyes met his, all he found was a well of sadness so profound it threatened to pull him under.

"Michelle…" Oliver started, his voice breaking on his sister's name. The word hung in the air, a specter none of them could escape.

"Oliver," Molly whispered, reaching across the table, her fingers hesitating just shy of his arm. "We…."

"Mom, it's okay," he interrupted, unsure if he was comforting her or himself.

Lisa watched the man she loved grappling with his pain; his shoulders were squared against the deluge of grief threatening to break through his carefully constructed dam. She felt the rawness of his soul laid bare, the boy who had lost his sister and now faced the ghosts of that loss head-on.

As they sipped their tea, each mouthful tasted of unspoken apologies and regrets. In the heart-wrenching silence that followed, the ticking of the clock on the mantel became a metronome to their collective heartbeat—a family united in sorrow, facing the remnants of a storm that had never truly passed.

❧

Molly's fingers were interlinked tightly in her lap, her knuckles whitened with the strain. John cleared his throat, a deep, rumbling sound that seemed to echo off the walls of the dimly lit living room.

"Oliver, there's not a day that goes by that we don't think about what happened to Michelle," John began, his voice thick with emotion. The timbre of regret in his voice was raw and palpable. "We had our disagreements, God knows, but we never imagined...."

"Your father and I," Molly interjected, her eyes brimming with unshed tears, "we thought she'd come back once things cooled down. We were so angry at the time, too proud to go after her." She looked up, her gaze meeting Oliver's. "We failed her as parents."

Oliver's chest tightened as he listened to the tremble in his mother's words and watched his father struggle to maintain composure. Their confessions were like shards of glass, each one piercing deeper into his heart. The shadows of the past seemed to cling to the edges of the room, whispering of missed opportunities and fractured relationships.

"Arguments happen in every family," Oliver said, his voice steady despite the whirlwind of emotions inside him. "But this… this silence for ten years. It's more than just pride, isn't it? She left and never even called any of us and never told us why."

Molly's lips parted, but no sound emerged. She glanced at John, seeking solace in his presence, but found none. They were united in their grief yet isolated by their own guilt.

"Son," John started, but Oliver cut him off with a raised hand. "We need to let it go. There's no use in ripping up the past; we can't…."

"No, Dad. No more excuses, no more secrets, and no more lies. I need to know what really happened to Michelle."

He stood abruptly, feeling a surge of adrenaline coursing through his veins. His chair scraped loudly against the wooden floor, an abrupt declaration of his intent.

"Oliver," Lisa said, reaching out to touch his arm, her expression filled with admiration and concern.

He turned to her, his blue eyes blazing with a fierce determination that belied the gentle nature she knew so well. "I'm not getting any answers here, Lisa. They'll never tell me the truth. I need to find it myself. For Michelle."

"Then we'll do it together," she replied, her voice

steady, though he could see the worry tugging at the corners of her smile.

Oliver nodded, grateful beyond words for her unwavering support. He faced his parents once more, his posture speaking of a man who would not be swayed from his course.

"Whatever it takes, I'm going to uncover the truth. Michelle deserves that much. We all do."

Outside, the sun dipped below the horizon, casting long shadows across the Thompsons' secluded home. Inside, as the last light of day faded, a new resolve took hold, propelling Oliver into the depths of a mystery that had lingered over their lives for far too long.

&

Gently closing the door behind them, Oliver and Lisa stepped out into the cooling twilight, their arms instinctively wrapping around each other. The world seemed eerily silent, save for the rustling of leaves in the breeze—a stark contrast to the heavy revelations that still echoed in their minds.

"God, I can't believe she's gone…" Oliver's voice trailed off as he clutched Lisa closer.

Lisa nestled her head against his chest, her presence a balm to the ache that had settled in his heart.

"We'll get through this," she murmured, her words muffled by his jacket.

As they reached the gravel driveway, pebbles crunching beneath their feet, Oliver stopped, looking back at the house that loomed in the fading light. It was as if the structure itself was burdened with untold stories, its windows reflecting not just the dying day but the ghosts of a past long hidden.

"Where do we even start?" Lisa asked with her gaze following his. Her hazel eyes, usually so warm, were now clouded with the weight of uncertainty.

"First, we need to find out where Michelle went after she left here." Oliver's hands were fists at his sides, the woodworker's callouses a testament to his ability to shape and fix things. But this wasn't wood; this was his life, and it would take more than skilled hands to put these pieces back together.

"Maybe someone in town knows something," Lisa suggested, her resilience shining despite the shadow of doubt. "Old friends, neighbors… there has to be someone who knows where she went."

"We could check social media, online records…" he trailed off, his mind racing with possibilities. There was a decade to cover in which Michelle could have built an entirely new life or met an untimely fate. They had searched for her back then but came up with nothing. He had never wanted to stop, but his parents had told him to let it go. He never should have listened to them.

"Let's start with what we know and go from there," Lisa said, her practicality grounding him as always. She pulled out her phone, tapping away to take notes. "We'll make a list tonight—people to talk to, places to visit, anything and everything that might lead us to her untold story."

Oliver gave a determined nod, feeling the stirrings of hope amidst the turmoil. "Whatever it takes."

They reached the police cruiser with Sheriff Coleman sitting in it, waiting for them. As Oliver opened the door for Lisa, he paused, allowing himself a moment to look into her eyes.

"Thank you," he whispered, the words thick with gratitude and love. "For being my partner in every sense."

"Always," she replied, squeezing his hand before sliding into the seat.

With one last glance at the darkened house, Oliver got into the car in the front seat next to the sheriff.

"You okay?" Sherriff Coleman asked.

Oliver nodded. "As okay as can be expected, I guess."

"It will get better," he said as the engine came to life with a soft purr.

"Oliver?" Lisa's voice broke through his reverie, laced with concern, as they stepped out of the cruiser and said goodbye and thank you to the sheriff.

"I know you said you were okay to the sheriff, but *are* you okay?"

He nodded, but his jaw clenched involuntarily. An urgency bubbled up inside him, the need for answers more pressing than ever.

Lisa reached out, her hand warm against his arm.

"We'll find the truth, Ollie. But we can't let it consume us."

"I need to know, Lisa." His words were fervent, an undercurrent of desperation threading through them. He shot her a look that bore the intensity of his resolve. "I need to understand why she vanished—why she didn't come back."

Her eyes softened, though worry creased her brow. "Just… don't lose yourself in this search," Lisa murmured, her fingers tracing patterns over his knuckles. The fierce determination in his gaze unsettled her; she knew the peril in obsession's grip all too well.

He nodded, though his heart raced with impatience. There was no turning back, not when the shadows of the past clung so tenaciously. "I won't," he promised, more to himself than to her. But the promise felt hollow against the magnitude of what lay ahead.

With a deep breath, Oliver turned his attention to the café in front of him, both their home and workplace. It looked different somehow now. A few hours ago, saving this place and making it work had been the most important task in his life. But now, everything had changed. It was no longer his number one priority. He had gained a new mission in life and was bracing his heart for whatever truths lay hidden in the darkness ahead.

End of excerpt.

Are you desperate to find out what happens to Lisa and Oliver next?
Get the third heart warming and captivating installment in the series, ***A Sister's Secret*** on Amazon.com

Books by the Author

THE FOREVER AND ALWAYS SERIES

- Book 1: ***The Lies We Live By***
- Book 2: ***The One That Got Away***
- Book 3: ***A Sister's Secret***

Contents

A SISTER'S SECRET